Penelope Gilliatt is the author of novels, short stories, plays and criticism and has also written an opera libretto commissioned by the English National Opera. Her past works include *Sunday Bloody Sunday* (the screenplay), *The Cutting Edge* and *A State of Change*. She divides her time between New York and England.

Penelope Gilliatt

MORTAL MATTERS

First published in Great Britain by
Macmillan London Limited 1983
Published in Abacus by
Sphere Books Ltd 1984
30–32 Gray's Inn Road, London WC1X 8JL
Copyright © 1983 by Penelope Gilliatt

Publisher's Note

Reproduced, printed and bound in Great Britain by
Hazell Watson & Viney Limited,
Aylesbury, Bucks

To William Shawn,
Vincent Canby,
and Nolan Osborne

MORTAL MATTERS

1

Galloping for all she might in the last quarter of our benighted century, Lady Corfe of Northumberland said mutely in her sleep at five in the morning, "We're not in *Northumberland,* we're being hauled to London. They're moving the house and all of us in it." Lady Corfe then immediately came to the surface, awakened by her own dream shouts for help, and pondered the question. She was as Northumbrian as her husband, a shipbuilder, now dead. Sir Andrew Corfe, on honeymoon with her in Italy, had signed his country of origin as "Northumberland." She was now in London, though, no question. She looked out of the window at the Georgian square, heard Big Ben. Builders' trestles and cranes and cement mixers were around the house everywhere. There was a piece of scaffolding under her window. A ruse to make a move, it still seemed. To tug her down south, a foreign land. To uproot her family from its given soil. Hellfire and no, she thought, and had a bath to bring her to her senses. Then she waited for the papers and coffee.

Out in the square, at five this morning, the silhouette of the house has been black against the dawn. Now it is six o'clock and the white stucco gleams. For a moment the façade comes

9

off in illusion and the house is like a doll's house with the door open. Activity is starting to burn. On the top floor, Lady Corfe writing letters on her knee. One below, her grandson Simon, climbing into stumped-off jeans and practicing on his skateboard to the ruination of the polished floor and possibly of his ankles or shins or knees, they being in the perpetually sprained or grazed condition of children. A floor below, Simon's mother, Eliza, beautifully asleep, and his father, Tony, presumed asleep in his dressing room, Eliza's grandmother's Cartier clock ticking in his void room (blue enamel and white marble with diamonds around the dial, a christening present from a Romanov to his grandmother-in-law, a French-speaking Scotswoman). His black velvet Dior evening slippers were neatly disposed under his orange Dior dressing gown on his Georgian rosewood cart-horse of a clothes rack. The slippers were embroidered in gold thread with his initials, AWC. To his wife's embarrassment and his mother's pang, the initials did not face the wearer but went the other way, to an audience. And then, descending, there was a floor of drawing rooms. And then the dining room and music room. And then the basement flat, where the Corfes' North-East married couple, Bill and Elsie, were starting breakfast. No mean breakfast for themselves, in spite of their age: they were a generation older than Tony and Eliza, taken into the house of Tony's mother when his father's death had caused them to be thrown out of the house by a mesmerist relation faint with self-pity. Bacon sizzled on the range. New bread was rising in the baking-oven on the left, some of it threaded into plaits of dough. Elsie's apron and arms were still floury and her wedding ring, which she chose never to take off, was caked to her fingers with flour.

"It says here in this advert, 'a diamond is for now,'" said Bill. "That's not what they told you in the old days, which is to say last month, times being what they are."

"It's not what I'd care for," said Elsie.

"A diamond is *forever.*"

"The bottom's dropping out of the market."

"Like upstairs."

"You driving for him today?"

"As per."

"Where to?"

"He hasn't told me, and anyway, that's his business."

"Come off it, Bill."

"I'm sorry for him."

"It's her I'm sorry for." Pause. "Or both."

"When am I going to get my bacon?"

"Hang on. I'm getting her tray ready, and some Chelsea espresso."

"Espresso! You're turning into a Londoner."

"Lady C. had to, and you can't say we don't owe her a lot."

Elsie gave them both some porridge and handed Bill the salt. Bill said, "Don't be daft, love. She's as North as we are for all she tries. She lives there in her head."

"You've noticed His Nibs takes sugar with his porridge now instead of salt. He would never have done that up North. Not when Lady Corfe was in the saddle."

"I seem to fancy sugar myself, this morning." So she passed him the sugar and said, "Put away your *Auto-Car,* then. No reading at breakfast. Even Simon knows that."

"He's a skinny lad. He could do with filling out. Time after time he doesn't have a lining to his stomach."

"It's not his mother's fault."

"Anyway he's generally up with Lady C. by this time, reading her papers."

"She hasn't got them yet. The bacon's ready."

"Simon slips down and nicks them for her."

"You're beginning to get a London flatness in your voice, Bill."

"It's natural, isn't it. Being here."

"The builders have come."

"Lovely sound of muck mixing."

"They do it neatly enough."

"To satisfy Her Highness," said Bill.

"That's rude, darling."

"Mrs. Corfe. Married to Mr. Corfe." Some acidity here, but Elsie loved him. So.

" 'Mr. Corfe,' " said Elsie. She put her hand on her husband's neck. "Tony, to us, knowing him since he was a little lad. She's not the one with airs. The builders are demanded by the insurers, she says, and she's worried about living too high. I found a pile of cost-of-living indexes in her wastepaper basket. I'd like to have everything nice for her. She's unhappy."

Bill whistled and ate his bacon and fried bread and said in his old Northumbrian voice, "Bye, they're making a bliddy clarton upstairs and we mustn't let arguments spread around here."

"That's what I was saying."

"Nice marmalade." He looked at the label on the jar and read her handwriting. "Nineteen-seventy-six, you made it. Matured in bottle, you might say."

The telephone rang. There was a row of phones on a disused Victorian ice-maker next door to a beautiful old treadle sewing machine. Elsie said, without turning, as builders started to crowd into the kitchen, "Is it his or hers?"

"Ours." Bill went to the row of telephones.

"Milk and two sugar for Dave the foreman and me, and coffee for the others," said a builder.

"Everything quite well, thank you," Bill said on the telephone.

"If you know so much, then, I mean if you think you know so much, you can find out for yourself, can't you? I told you.

12

The whole family is here and none of them speaks to reporters. I couldn't say. Yes, the *whole* family. I said whole, didn't I? Excuse me, but we're having breakfast."

Elsie said to the foreman builder, "Milk and sugar with all the coffee, is it now? There are two of you new I haven't met."

"This is Nick and I'm Alan," said one of the new builders.

"How long is this chaos going to go on, then?"

"Plaster takes two weeks to dry out," said Dave.

"Who was that?" Elsie said to Bill; and to the builder, "We could turn the central heating on if it wasn't for the oil emergency. It's like a time of war, isn't it. I could give you my hair dryer. We've got a dinner tonight and I'd like to see the portico done."

"If you've got a blow-heater. We'd have to get an extension cord from Nick."

"It was that bastard journalist with the good manners again," said Bill across Elsie about the phone call.

"I'd forgotten it was the end of the month. Reporters must have it in their diaries to ring people every end of the month. You'd think they'd get bored, gossip about people they don't know."

"He says he knows where Mister's been and who with and he wants to know any rows here."

"That's the thing about couples like them, they don't actually have rows, do they? Just tears on their own." Elsie waited over the bacon. "Poor mites."

"It's him I'm sorry for."

"He'd try the patience of the Queen. If he hadn't had that nanny. She's redundant. If you think that Mrs. Corfe doesn't even let her near Simon, for good reason. Hilda eating her head off up there and thinking any grown man she's had the charge of, Mr. Corfe being the one in question, can't do any-

13

thing wrong. No, that's all right, Fred, there's always plenty of milk. You look as if you've been driving all night in the desert, covered with plaster, white as a sheet. Which reminds me, you owe me five of my dust sheets." The house phone.

"You answer it, Bill."

"It's *her* house phone."

"Just on the way up, madam. I haven't asked Mr. Corfe yet. Bill's just off to pick something up for him. I don't know where." Elsie saw the builders upstairs.

"Best get on with it." When she came down again, she said, "It's the first time I've ever known her to come out with a question before about her own husband's whereabouts. Awake on and off all night as usual, I expect."

"No sense in your living other people's lives."

"I can't help fretting."

"If you do that you'll get thin, and then what'll I do?"

Elsie gave him a piece more bacon and then prepared three trays to go upstairs. One with an espresso machine and a cup and saucer and napkin, another with tea and fried eggs and toast and butter and milk and sugar and a napkin, the third with a napkin, hot water, and a lemon slice. For Eliza Corfe, Hannah, and Lady Corfe. All with salt and pepper on them.

Bill said, "I don't know why you bother with the napkins and the salt and pepper. Not with espresso coffee only, or worse still with hot water and lemon."

"I wish she'd have an egg. It's not right."

"And Lady Corfe could be doing with one."

"She's not had anything but hot water and lemon for thirty years."

The house phone went. "That'll be the hungry gorgon," said Bill. "Yes, Hannah, it'll be on its way in a moment." And then,

14

to Elsie, "Give her three scrambled eggs and warm up Dave's tea and send her my *Auto-Car.*"

"You might need it. You enjoy the classified ads."

"Put a few biscuits on Lady Corfe's tray."

"She'd only leave them. Old people can go for days without food, like boa constrictors. It's Mrs. Corfe that needs building up."

Bill washed up his bacon-and-egg plate and said, "The whole house is starving itself. I never get over people with money. They have enough to eat anything they want and then they deprive themselves." Elsie put the trays on the food lift and wound the lift up to the main bedroom floor, following it up and letting Hannah's cooked breakfast do what it might. She took the espresso-coffee tray into Eliza's room. Bill left a tea tray for Tony outside the dressing-room door with a copy of *The Financial Times* and *The Wall Street Journal* and *The Hartlepool Chronicle* in the hope that he would be back before Eliza knew the present train of fibs, not paltry. Bill was glad the house still took the old local Hartlepool paper. Some sense there, at least.

A week later the same circumstances reigned, except that the façade of the shapely house seemed to be in more disrepair than ever, and there were to be more calls from builders and the backboned Eliza and the steadying Lady Corfe for tea and coffee than ever. "They're turning a Georgian house into a Tudor relic," said Elsie to Bill, again at five in the morning, the outline of the house moving from silhouette into dimension as the sun came up. After the sizzling of the griddle pan while she was making griddle cakes for Bill, old breakfast habits being at least something to hang on to, the telephone went again.

"His or hers?" again.

"Ours," again.

"Maybe the garage."

"Chance would be a fine thing."

"No, he's off skiing," said Bill to the telephone.

"Skiing?" said Elsie into the griddle pan.

"I'm meeting them," said Bill. "London, I said. He's long ago left the North. That's all I have to say. I can't give you the time."

"He shouldn't ever have left the North," Elsie said to him. "Nor should we."

"We're with them."

"With her and him, you might say," said Elsie. Then Elsie, who had merriment, ladled griddle cakes onto both their plates and said, "Well, if it wasn't for this griddle, this *girdle*"—no right to inflict change onto us on top of everything else—"if it wasn't for this girdle iron and its weight I'd be throwing one of our cakes at you, hinny. And where are you going to?"

"London Airport after his business trip, I said."

"I'm not a meddler. That's not how we earn our money. Get him fast, hinny. She knows he wasn't at London Airport. Silly messing around. We've all got jobs to do, luckily. Though you've got offers from gossip people to fend off, and you've got the petrol and telephone calls to look after."

Bill ate his griddle cakes. "They're fine, hinny," he said. "You're looking bonny today. Doing anything nice for her?"

"I thought I'd go to the greengrocer and get her an avocado for lunch."

"She'd only be having half an avocado. Who's the other half for?"

"Mr. Gould. I'll do something hot for Lady Corfe."

"*Dick* Gould, that Newcastle singer. New*cassle*. At least he said it right," said Bill.

"Composer. He's risen in the world. He's been recognized. And then I thought toad-in-the-hole and haggerty, to remind them where they come from. Though they've moved away from there."

"Moved on is what you mean, like us." Bill wiped his mouth with Elsie's apron and clasped her around her knees. "It's happened to all of us. Both lots of us."

"Not to me. Not to Lady Corfe. Only to *him*, who you say you're meeting at London Airport or wherever you mention." Pause. "Want to mention."

"London Airport."

There was another long pause while Elsie busied herself about the locker of frozen food and inspected the larder.

"Lovely lot of things you've got ready," said Bill.

"If I could get them to eat. At Lady Corfe's age it's understandable, but at Mr. Corfe's age his breakfast isn't manly. Is the car shined? He's living above his rights."

"Who do you think I am, hinny?" Bill lifted Elsie above his waist. "I know how he likes his car."

"The Bentley is his choice of car. She'd like a secondhand jeep for her sculpture tools."

Bill dropped her down. "It's his money."

"And she wants to drive her mum-in-law after she's been to the foundry and finished her work. Take His Nibs a cold girdle-cake sandwich with some of the honeycomb when you get him back. It's what he always used to fancy."

Bill drove past the turning to London Airport, he wearing chauffeur's uniform and gloves, to a house labeled Nettledown Health Farm. It was a diet farm of opulence. Patients were wandering about in dressing gowns, carrying glasses of soda water with lemon peel, looking hungrily at a dining room where advanced patients were having meals of the same soda water and the same lemon slices with a plateful sparsely arranged with an olive and grated carrot. The women guests were not made up. Their dressing gowns were not worn with dash. Bill spoke to a woman behind the reception desk: a woman of department-store-buyer type, everything under one roof, everything from a harpsichord to an elephant. People were lying about in armchairs, deep armchairs that robbed them of any energy they had left, lugging themselves up as if they weighed more than ever after all this effort, or sunk in a famished coma. Many of them were looking in a passionate way at recipe books and food advertisements. There was an impression of ordinarily rapid beings in water chemicalized to idle them into lifelessness and at the same time to inject them with fallacious coloring: food-free, polyunsaturated, artificially carbonated coloring. People seemed poised as if for death, not for the life they had come here for in such expensive hope.

A porter suited like a male nurse went up the stairs and into a bedroom door. He came out shortly with luggage, followed by Mr. Corfe, with a limp and a stick, trailed by a fashion-shaped girl called Georgina. One of Tony's feet was in plaster. He was forty, Harrovian, unlike his son, Simon, who was at Eton. For all the purpose and achievements of the slimming farm, he was already lean enough, one would have thought. He had a look of almost oppressive fitness and a neighing laugh. His girlfriends were all much like Georgina: pretty, overbred, silenced by a fear that they did not put down to their drugs and their aimlessness, sufficiently egocentric not to impinge on him much, young enough to interest him in their lives ahead rather as he would be rapt by the racing future of one of the yearlings he bred. Georgina was an especially ravishing new runner to take about. She was also particularly self-absorbed. Even Tony discerned it. She was sobbing. At the top of the stairs, he said to her, stopping in his tracks, "I'm sure you're only crying because you haven't had enough to eat."

Georgina was wearing becoming dark glasses steamed up with tears. "No. I could do days more of this. It's just like home. Anyway, I haven't lost anything like as much weight as you because they said I haven't got it to lose. I'm not really crying. I mean, I'm only crying because it's over. I always do that at the end of everything. I used to when I was a little girl at the circus."

Endings, departures.

He said, "After every act?"

Fascinated by his interest, not usual, she said, "Yes, every single act. The trapeze and the lions and the elephants and everything. They all made me feel so sad. Bears in ballet skirts. It's like these people. Rich beautiful people in tawdry dressing gowns. You're not listening."

"Dreaming of steak."

"Poor darling, and I feel marvellous. I never eat much. If I've stopped making you feel drab it's been like a honeymoon, hasn't it? Private and expensive."

"I should hope so," said Tony, paying the bill while Georgina watched the hall full of people lying like stranded fish gasping for breath on dry land, other people rising with a struggle in an anteroom where a gong was sounding for turnip juice. "They look like dolphins coming up out of the water being taught to speak," she said.

"Get into my car, won't you?" said Tony. "My Mamma's waiting."

"You didn't tell me."

"Why should I?"

In the back of the car, they talked as though Bill were not there. Georgina said, "I'm frozen."

"It's the lack of calories."

"What are you going to eat today?"

"Proteins and alcohol."

"Your businessman's diet. On a businessman's diet I'd gain. I'd be enormous."

"Bill, drop Miss Hargreaves off fast."

She fell silent. Bill thought she was incapable of feeling. But the stripe of darkness was on here. "Let *me* drop *you*," she said. Tony didn't answer. He was reading papers in folders.

"You're first. Do let *me*," she said. Pause. "I've got nothing else to do." Pause. "Do you like your mother?"

"She prefers Eliza, because Eliza's Socialist godmother was my Tory godfather's first Minister of Agriculture and Fisheries. I've got a lot of time for anyone who was in my godfather's Cabinets. Particularly his first Cabinet. Or indeed for anyone who has really achieved anything. Whereas she treats me as if being in insurance were like being in tomato ketchup. Home Counties tomato ketchup, making a packet out of Tyneside unemployed."

"I asked you if you liked her, not if she liked you."

"It's the same thing."

"Do you really think that? How intriguing." Pause.

"Would I like Eliza? I realize she can't possibly like me."

"She hardly knows you exist. You don't concern her." They passed Sadler's Wells ballet school near St. Paul's schoolyard. Georgina said, "What are you thinking about? Dividends? On what was it you were talking about yesterday? Somebody's shortfall?" Pause. "Or us?"

"Food. I don't feel very well."

"You're only the second unwell Harrovian I've ever met." Chatter, to prolong the journey. "The other's called George Haltwhistle."

"I'd have remembered the name."

"All the hypochondriacs I know were at Winchester. Two are photographers. You wouldn't have met them either. I mean, you're not going to now, not unless you come to dinner. You aren't listening."

"It isn't good for the system to clear out all the poisons and then sit in the back breathing petrol fumes. Petrol is toxic. It must be. In fact, I should have thought that petrol is probably just as disastrous as polyunsaturated fats. As far as the body is concerned."

Tony read more figures, but they meant little to him in his concerns about his racing pulse, which he measured against his Cartier waterproof watch. "I thought so, tachycardia. Rapid pulse. This watch was a good choice, sweetie. Thank you."

"Darling," she said, "it's been like a honeymoon. I'm glad you like your present. I got it for you on your account." Guileless, she thought he would reach for her hand, but he was sorting papers. He said, "I don't mean to be casual, Georgina, but I've got a lot on my mind, trying to catch up."

"It must be an odd change of world. I mean, nobody having known where you were, and now there'll be lists of people to call, pinning you down."

"Perhaps I shouldn't have lost so much weight. Nanny always said I have big bones. People in the South have bigger bones than in the North, she says. She's got mighty bones herself. Much bigger than my Mamma's."

"The only other nanny I've ever known is made like a bird. She's from Chalfont St. Giles."

"How funny. Mine has a sister who lives in Chalfont St. Peter's." It was the first time for the whole while that they had been in the car that Tony had looked at Georgina, his pretty Georgina.

"Perhaps they should meet, living so near. I wonder if they'd get on?"

"Darling Georgina, nannies always get on. It's like black African prime ministers or heads of state. It's simply not workable that they shouldn't get on. Politics is the art of the—no, life is the politics of the workable." He took note of the muddled aphorism he had uttered, finding it good.

"Eliza would have laughed then," he said.

Georgina, rash enough to risk things by looking amused, then kissed him, saying, "You're sweet when you whine."

He became the iron chairman.

"You don't upset me a bit when you talk about Eliza, you know. You probably hope you do. Mistresses do."

"I'm not mistresses."

"I know, sweetie, you're Georgina. You mustn't cry, little Georgina." He made a face about the pain in his foot and said, "I wouldn't dream of your dropping me. It's right on the way. You'll have your own laundry list of calls to deal with."

"There's been nobody to take them. What do I say if people ask me where we've been?"

"We?"

"You can't think that people don't know, when we've been to the opera and Crockford's and the VIP lounge at London Airport. I don't understand. We're not invisible. I'm proud of you. I'm sure Eliza would probably rather you told the truth. How are you going to explain the foot, for instance?"

"The truth, as you said. A skiing accident."

"Alone? I can't deal with your cover-ups, Tony. Get to work."

"International bankers?"

"Just don't fret your wife."

He said, "There's something ghoulish about the way mistresses identify with the wives they're supposed to hate. Do stop trying to live other people's lives. Concentrate on having as many lives as you can yourself."

"Why not one?"

Bill had to slow for a traffic light and Georgina said, "Can we stop here?"

Tony said nothing, but Bill halted. Georgina ran into a newsagent's and bought herself a load of women's magazines and then a packet of Maltesers, four bars of chocolate, and a packet of wine gums. Tony took a brief look and then back at his folders. He dropped her off. She let herself into her upstairs flat with her case and newsagent's provisions. They were provisions as if for going up Everest. She sat down on a water bed that she had bought with Tony in some fling of unreality after lunching at the White Tower on taramosalata and moussaka, such foreign foods that she had to pretend to find them hospitable. Where did this man come from? Northumberland, he had always said. But from everywhere and nowhere. Taramosalata was no more Northumbrian than shark's fins.

The place served Turkish or Italian or Kona coffee, the waiter had said.

"I'm glad I'm not Konese," she had said to Tony.

"What?" he had said, not one to understand failed attempts at lightness.

"And what?" he had said again as he had dropped her. "You're cross because I can't get out to see you upstairs? For Christ's sake, I have got this foot."

She nodded and ran upstairs to eat Maltesers, crying, and putting them in the fridge along with the other chocolates. There was little else in the fridge. Jam, chutney, an old croissant; some of his tobacco, which he said improved if it was kept chilled. In the nonsense of loneliness she put her magazines there too and went to have a bath and do her hair before keeping an appointment with a magazine photographer.

At the Corfes' house, Elsie met Bill with a swift exchange of difficulty and took Tony's briefcase. The white plaster around his foot, that morning whitened with tennis-shoe polish, was irredeemably demanding of sympathy.

"Sir, what have you done?"

"I broke it on a step. Going to a conference." He went up bravely. "Blasted painful. Don't worry Her Ladyship."

"I hope it was interesting, sir. Abroad. Apart from the foot."

"Hard work."

"Mrs. Corfe's upstairs. With Lady Corfe and Simon."

"North and South. Simon and I have adjusted, eh."

"A world of difference."

"There's a lot to be gained in the financial capital of the world; though it's another life, I appreciate."

"There's something lacking, sir."

"Take my things up if you would and I'll attend to the post in the study. The post is in the study, of course?"

He went on up, making heavy weather of his foot, gave himself a large Scotch and soda, propped the white-plastered foot on his desk, and skimmed through one of his office folders, looking sympathetically at his foot between letters. It didn't occur to him for quite a while to seek out the people awaiting him in the drawing room half a landing away; people including his wife.

Lady Corfe was standing in front of the long French windows with a sherry, rocking herself on her heels with a silver-headed cane in her right hand. Simon was playing rock on the harpsichord for Eliza. Lady Corfe was talking to Eliza, speaking of a cousin of hers, a magistrate who had come down South.

"She's hardened. When she's on the bench she does her best to give a boy six months at the least."

"It seems a bit much just for cheating on the tube," said Lady Corfe.

"All too many have done it " said Eliza. "It's made us Dickensian pickpockets. What would this cousin of yours like to do? I know her a little. Mend matters, I hope? No, when push comes to shove I suppose she'd really like to bring back the press gangs and send offenders to another fabricated war like the Falkland Islands."

"Jingoism. She's not to your sort of liking, Eliza. She has a bobbed haircut that she calls Bobbity, after Lord Salisbury,

24

whom she didn't know, of course, but she fancies the association. I'm afraid she's regrettable. She lives in Henley with a regatta of a family and never does she stop reminding you of the fact. I sometimes think that if I hear her instructing another American in Leander rowing-club pink socks and Leander pink ties, an American from Harvard or somewhere who's obviously been elected to Leander as no upstart, I'll cut off family relations. Not that she'd notice. She does it to all the non-English but especially to Americans. I feel like throwing tea into the Thames on their behalf. The United States is a continent where nearly everyone elected to be American. Unique. We were merely born here. Small country. Most people in the United States just don't understand that there's a difference between Northumberland and the South."

"If they've ever heard of the Border, they associate it with Border raids a thousand years ago. But God knows we planted the Celts in Ulster before Cromwell, and it's here in the South that we're getting the IRA bombings. Mini. Violence about borders is all over the world. We need a periscope from Mars to understand this planet. Thank the Lord I'm not a Head of State."

They went on to talk of politics. Lady Corfe said out of the blue, "I was reading Russian last night, and it occurred to me that the most interesting piece of dialogue in all Chekhov, and to my shame I can't remember where I read it, is when a character very late at night says to a friend, 'Onward, onward,' and he waves a pickled herring, and then he says 'But the question is, in what direction?' It strikes me very much, that." She put aside her cane and went over to Simon, who was stumbling over a difficult piece on the harpsichord, and said, "Let the left hand do that part on the upper manual or else you're in thumb trouble." Coming back again, she said to Eliza gently, with Tony at the root of her words, "How's life?"

"Getting on."

"How's your sculpture going?"

"Poorly," said Eliza. The women had much in common: most of all, their capacity to speak of their worrisome Tony while apparently speaking of other things. Mother and daughter-in-law, neither of them traitors.

"That should be all right if you know it. People aren't buying? You mean the recession. It's not you."

Eliza stood at the window, feeling desolate at the sight of the absurd parked Bentley below. "The car's here," she said to the room. "But usually he'd have come up and found me."

"Don't fool yourself." Lady Corfe said many things softly. She went to the row of house telephones and dialled a few rooms. "I can't find Elsie or Bill. I expect he's gone straight to the office. He'll telephone."

"This house he wanted is too big. Try his study," said Eliza, "just in case he's in and has some reason for not coming up."

Below, Tony looked obstinately at his house telephone and failed to answer it.

"We were going to have lunch," said Eliza. "We were. All of us were. He's bound to come in soon."

Needing some solitude urgently, she whispered to Simon to keep his alert grandmother occupied and went upstairs. She changed, looked at herself in the looking glass, disliked what she saw and changed back again. Then she dialled the basement, and then the nursery, getting Hannah, who was no gorgon to her.

"Where's Elsie?" she said to the old lady, who was crocheting. "Did she say anything about Mr. Corfe? I wasn't asking you to repeat gossip. Hold your hush, dear one. Come down and have coffee."

After a time of thought she went to the window, and then to Tony's side of the bed, opening his bedside drawer and looking at piles of socks and shirts and tennis sweaters. She found some old Callard and Bowser toffee beside bottles of vitamin pills and ate a piece. Then she went to the outside telephone and dialled Dick Gould.

"You asked me to remind you. I promised your mother you'd ring. She said she was fine to me and she could get along the block easily, as she had her oxygen cylinder going. You sound as if I've woken you. I've found a fine holiday for you if it's worth affording. No, I'm not coming. I read about it in one of the papers this morning. They've got some process in France that puts you to sleep for a fortnight. I think it's really to cure melancholia or to let the unconscious learn Japanese, but even though you're anti-melancholic and anti-Japanese I'm sure it would be a good idea. You've got two jobs going and that's through effort and you're worn out. Hanging around for the other life to happen is no life at all. I'm having a go with Tony on the same lines."

Dick said, "So he's back. Again. Don't get excited."

"This other life, I think they call it. No, I know he isn't excited, but I am."

"Don't deceive yourself," said Dick, feeding a pet monkey on his shoulders with the banana that the monkey peculiarly liked.

"I know I sound as if I am, but the only way to resolve it would be to get angry."

"He's having an affair."

"The only way to resolve it would be to get angry, as I said, and I don't seem to feel angry, only exhilarated about you and me, and happy about seeing him."

"Happy about attrition."

"Yes. Though I know you don't approve of not making clean breaks. Any good offering to ring your mother for you? No, no one can deal with any one else's mother for them."

"Say that to Simon."

"I know I'm a mother too. It's probably a doomed thing to be. I think of it every time Simon talks to me. Though not today. He was having a good time with the harpsichord, and his grandmother plays it." Eliza stared at a photograph of Simon beside her bed. She went on to say, "Would you like me to come round? When you wake up? Why don't we go to Northumberland with Simon? No, that wouldn't be right, I suppose. Don't forget to ring your old mum." She lay on the bed a long time and then dialled on the house phone to every room and eventually found Tony.

"Darling, you're back," she shouted. "Hang on."

She ran to find a wrapped present in her drawer, and then down to his study. At the sight of his Wimbledon-white plastered foot on his desk, she stopped, mustered, and said, "What's happened?"

"I broke a bone on a step. Going to a conference. A conference about bank rates."

"It said on the news that you'd had a skiing accident but I couldn't get through to anyone sensible. You've got very brown. Which hospital?"

"I'd been in Zurich. Drinking hot chocolate in the snow all day with international bankers." Pause. Tony swallowed. "After the accident, that was, but international bankers don't ski. They sit at the bottom of the ski lift."

She said, "A suntan that you've got from Manly Tan looks a bit different from getting brown in the snow, darling."

"Men don't seem to possess suspiciousness as adequately as womankind. We possess prowess."

"I suppose it shows that you do if you say so easily that you do. But prowess is not much of a gift. It's a very random attribute."

"Your harassing composure."

"There you go. Showing pain to you always invites reprisals."

"My foot," he said, speaking of another kind of pain.

It's my pain, she heard him saying, but in spite of that heard herself saying, "Does it hurt a lot?"

"To be fair, less than you think and more than you'd wish." He put down his fountain pen, aware of his fairness, and said to her, "I must go upstairs and get changed for lunch."

"Where shall we go?"

"I'm taking Simon to the club."

"What about your Mamma? She was looking forward to having lunch with all of us."

"You take her somewhere. I want to get Simon off the hook of punk on the harpsichord and also to do something about that disc-jockey voice of his. You simply must talk to his tutor about it."

"Half Eton has it. The most interesting half. It's their private language for getting out of those undertaker's clothes. Same as you speaking words backwards at Oxford, or was it ending every word with a peculiar extra syllable?"

"Talking backwards was quite different. That was an invention. Simon is copying."

"Mickey says if you send a boy to Eton he's bound to come out oddly one way or another and we can be thankful it's only a peculiar way of speaking."

"Your queens' truisms. The thing I hate about half the people you see is that you bring their truisms into the house."

"Not half, only Mickey."

"I gather from Elsie that Mickey's coming here today."

"This truism thing. You make your truisms sound an ailment like rheumatism or astigmatism. Anyway, Mickey isn't aphoristic, he's mostly loyal. I only meant that mid-Atlantic just sounds peculiar to some of us. It's no more odd than your saying 'harry-aggers' when you mean 'agonizing.' Is it? Shouldn't you stay in and have lunch with your foot up?"

"No, one's got to get going. Unlike Mickey."

29

"Why are you vicious about queens?"

"They're fickle."

She was a little staggered at the news of that and waited a moment before saying, "That's not true."

"They also get away with murder. No school bills and no alimony."

"Mickey's one of the most generous men I know."

Pause.

"Sometimes your pauses, darling," said Eliza.

"I'm simply straightening my bandage."

Tony went on fiddling to no visible purpose and said, "Even your working-class layabouts like Dick are preferable to the queens you go around with."

"Not 'queens.' *Mickey*. He's one of my closest friends and it's absurd not to use his name."

"I'd rather you were having ten affairs."

"That can't be true, can it? Dear one, that can't be true?"

"As long as you didn't insist on confessing."

"I can see there'd be no point. In making the effort, if you didn't care anyway."

"Exactly."

"Darling, I'm only having one. The same one as ever, and not often. I don't flaunt it. Elsie doesn't know, your Mamma seems not to. Though she's canny, but she keeps her silence. Not in the way you do. She just knows how not to ask. Simon certainly doesn't know."

"Dick the Geordie piper. It's such a ludicrous profession."

"He started as a plumber, that's why the pipes. You've never understood about Northumbrian pipes. They're not bagpipes or French horns, they're an invention by very musical people."

"It's still funny."

"Also he's a nice man. And scrupulous."

"Well, live with him, then."

"Do you want to divorce me? Oh, no, darling?"

"I don't think so. You run the house rather well. And it would be bad for what our American cousins call my image."

"Oh God."

"Now what?"

"You're always bantering. I can't ever get you to be serious any longer."

"You're losing your sense of humuor." At last he looked at her face and was moved.

"I meant serious, not solemn," said Eliza.

"Surely you know I won't have a wife who can't take things lightly." Return to flippancy. Behind his back, Eliza beat her fists against her thighs for a moment. He was staring at his foot.

"Is it very painful?" she said.

"It is rather."

"I suppose it's lucky it's not worse. Skiing accidents."

"Accidents on slippery steps, professional accidents on the way to conferences you've never seen the like of—"

"Any sort of accident can be bad, like drowning in five inches of water." Eliza put her arms around his neck from behind. "That's what we're doing."

"Do you mind leaving me? I've got a telephone call."

"Will you come up?"

"In a moment."

She looked at his foot. "Can you manage the stairs on your own?"

"I told you, I've got to be alone."

She shut the door behind her. He dialled a number.

"Georgina, do you want to have lunch? I'm taking Simon, and Eliza's rather deserted me. She seems to have twigged about the skiing weekend but not about the health jaunt. No. She's all right when she's being amusing but it really is too gruesome when she's on a crying jag. Nothing for you to worry about. No, she'd never dream of lawyers, she's not reckless. One doesn't throw everything away at thirty-four."

He sat at his desk still and then dialled the basement.

"Bill, I'd like you to drive Mrs. Corfe today. I'll take taxis. No, use mine, it's more comfortable for her. Anyway, I wouldn't be able to park mine anywhere."

Again he dialled Georgina.

"I've told Bill to drive Eliza today, as a sort of penance. You know. And I wondered if you'd like to drive me to the office after lunch in your car? And then bring me back again. Only three or four hours. You could look at the Mansion House or something. Taxis are going to be difficult with my foot, and it looks like rain." Upstairs in his dressing room he said to Eliza, groaning with careful mildness, "Darling, I want you to have my car, and Bill. For today, I mean. The *whole* day."

"How will you manage?"

"Will you ask Elsie to go out and get me two walking sticks?"

"I can't possibly have a chauffeur-driven car when you're a cripple."

"I'm not a cripple. One leg is fine and the other is numb anyway with pain."

"Where do I buy sticks? Elsie's busy."

"Harrods, I should think. Or Chelsea Red Cross; you could get them free there."

"Surely people who are well off shouldn't use the Red Cross."

"I am the Chairman."

Muted as usual, she looked at his mesmerizing foot. "How do you manage to keep the plaster so white? I thought casts always got filthy. You're the only man I know who could look debonair with his foot in plaster."

32

"I have it done with Blanco."

"Like tennis shoes. You mean you'll leave it outside your bedroom door every night for Bill to do? He's got the logs and the car to see to. I wouldn't put it past you to have two specially detachable casts, one for bed. Or three, knowing you. One on, one off, and one in the wash, like Simon's school sweater. It must have been a very grand hotel you were in, to be up to Blancoing a plaster cast."

"Well, yes, it was."

"I hope the foot will be better for you when you go off for your wildflowers. You must do a lot of walking, looking for wildflowers."

"Are you being caustic?"

"Not a bit. How could I be caustic with you, my dove, going off to Switzerland every summer with your great-uncle's fishing bag to hunt for wildflowers? I mean, one can't. The feat itself is too . . . er . . ."

"What?"

"Engaging. Barmy. You know I think that."

A few minutes later Tony was standing on one leg in front of his Edwardian shaving stand and trying a Windsor knot in another tie. Eliza was on her knees to the other leg, touching up his plaster with a bit of Blanco.

"Actually Georgina happened to be in Switzerland and she skied a little. After this accident at the conference, I mean. You're not on a crying jag again, are you?"

"How was she?"

"Marvellous. She was very good to me about the blessed foot. She's a sympathetic girl about pain. I don't think she's very well herself, actually. In fact neither of us was. I think she's nervous. She comes out in a rash on her chest. Sometimes."

"Now who's insisting on confessing."

Eliza was indeed crying now. She recovered herself and said,

"I'm sorry, darling, I hate tit for tat." Enough, she said to herself. So she put away the Blanco in the medicine cupboard and said, "I wonder if Blanco would be any good for red eyes. I loathe myself looking like this. Perhaps she should see a doctor about her allergies?"

"I'm sending her to Maxwell."

"Darling, Maxwell's both our doctor and he's getting confused. You've already sent Annabel to him, and Françoise, and who was the one you thought had an ulcer? Belinda."

"There no reasonable reason, no *rational* reason, why Georgina shouldn't have whoever I consider the best practitioner available, just as you have."

"Maxwell's an old friend of ours and it makes it awkward for him."

"The best medical practitioner, just as you have, as I said."

"Yes."

"Petty jealousy shouldn't enter into the Hippocratic oath."

"No."

"This is a question of health. I said, she's a very nervous girl, and very gifted, like her father."

She washed her face and said, "You did always say that. That she took after her father and that he hadn't got a working nerve in his body. In fact he's the most arrogant man we've ever had to dinner. He has that absolutely false modesty which only the numbest English pushers have and which seems to come from eating polite aliens and other ranks alive. It's like what they always say about English lawns: only five hundred years of mowing and rolling could produce that sort of perfection at how to be crushing while a brute is looking shy. I should think his ancestors were modestly eating noncommissioned officers and other upstarts for breakfast at the Battle of Hastings. What does he do? I forget."

"Chairman of Aztec razor blades."

"Oh, yes."

"Among other things. And he took a double first at Balliol. And you know he has that rather brilliant son. That tailor."

"The one who looks like Anthony Eden at Munich?"

"Yes, you could say."

"Except that I don't think he's had a moment of political uncertainty in his life. The uncertainty would certainly be there, though, it would be a rare person—"

"Could you be an angel and forage for those sparkling vitamin-C tablets for me?"

"I suppose tailoring off your own bat is pretty gallant, given Aztec."

"All right, carry on arguing with yourself."

"Oh darling, I'm sorry, but I think I finished the fizzy stuff myself one night last week."

"For God's sake, I can't even have vitamins in my own house."

"Would an aspirin help?"

"I want a vitamin pill, not an aspirin. What are you looking at?"

"Your new watch."

"None of your business."

"It's handsome. It's new."

Eliza put the watch on his shaving stand and said, having just bought him a new watch herself, "I'm sorry."

"Do stop being sorry."

Pause. "It isn't very good, darling, is it? We're not together enough any longer to be properly mended. Often you're sweet and pretend to be having fun with me to keep our spirits up. Yet you don't want a divorce, for some reason, and I don't, because you're beloved. So we end up using convention to be unkind to each other."

He said, "The old watch you gave me is being repaired. Or something. It's just gone somewhere. Oh Lord, it's raining. I wonder how busy you'll really be with Bill."

35

"Your Mamma and I can always have an egg at home, but I was thinking about his having enough time to get your sticks."

In the basement, Elsie said to Bill, who was putting on his cap, "So you'll be taking His Nibs out to lunch."

"With Simon."

"Where are you going?"

"I'll be told. Best not to ask me."

"We can't stop talking to each other just because they're having difficulties."

"Now that he's changed his mind about lending her the car, there'll be lunch for you to get here," as Elsie put on her waterproof cap and a pair of waterproof booties.

"I'm going out to get some stuff for a curry. They'll be fed up with my sausages and mash and cottage pie."

"You could be reading up on soufflés in the evening. You've got enough cookery books to keep a lending library."

"Not soufflé; it's a difficulty in a range. I'll make them a lemon sorbet to follow."

At the back door, Elsie turned round and said to her husband, "However did he wangle his way out of his promise about the car? He had a face like a meat axe."

"I expect he was feeling guilty. Guilt turns the milk sour."

"He's got a temper today you'd need an umbrella for."

"No wonder she's been crying."

"She's upset about him."

"It's what they've chosen, isn't it?" said Bill, making a move to peel some onions for her and then going back to his morning paper.

"What were you doing then?"

"Thinking of peeling an onion or two for upstairs. Sausages and mash or shepherd's pie or curry, whatever it is they'd come in. I like the way you do them."

"What stopped you?"

"I didn't want tears in my eyes, they stop me reading the football."

"It's the football pools that make me cry."

"Anyway, I haven't got your knack, peeling onions under a running tap. We haven't had running water that long, my girl."

"No time for the pools in the days when we had the pump. Gallons to fill the tub in front of the range."

"It's the range they've got here that attracted me to the place, and we don't need to start a clart-on about who does what."

Elise looked at him fondly and pulled her mackintosh hat around her ears after laying a plastic cover over her shopping basket to keep it dry.

"Next time it comes to this without raining I'll take Simon's pram. It's got a lovely hood for groceries and it's not doing anybody any good in the larder. Once the pride of Kensington Gardens."

Upstairs, later, over the curry, Lady Corfe said to Eliza, "I think I'll go home for a while. We've been away from the North for too long. There's trouble between you and Tony, isn't there?"

"Yes. No worse than a little."

"There shouldn't be any, and it's infecting Elsie and Bill. They'll be splitting up in a bad way if you don't see the danger. The trouble is Tony, I'm afraid. It doesn't do to come South in the case of a weak man."

"What a terrible thing for a mother to say. For a mother to have to say."

"We only need to get our bearings."

2

L ady Corfe got into the night sleeper to Newcastle. Every time she had come South in her life, she had taken a day train down and the night sleeper back. There was some feeling of a mission accomplished in doing it that way, of setting out for battle and coming back to the known and trustworthy. In the old days the sleeping compartment had been beautiful: old brass fittings and mahogany furniture, with a basin that pulled out of one corner. The bed would be freshly made up with the top sheet turned back for her. It was an invitation to read, to experiment with lamps designed after the fashion of gas lamps, to lapse into a coma of fatigue after exams. The train now had a taint of plastic about it in the furnishings, but the service remained. The night-sleeper porter, her butler for the journey, asked when she wanted to be woken with tea and biscuits. She preferred coffee, and he could even do it, as well as her hot water, though not the lemon. The sheets were fresh as Northumbrian air, as ever, and the lights were in the right place for reading and dressing. She read the familiar train document about the stately programme of events and services. She had books in her luggage, but word-minded people will read even the nonsense on the side of a cereal package if it happens to be facing them at some moment of suspension. The wording was blessedly unchanged. The times were the same for being allowed to linger on the train at both ends of the journey. Most important, there remained the clause about the drugget. Her drugget, said the notice, could be found stowed under the bed. From years of sleeper train travel she knew that it was a hemmed piece of laundered cotton to be spread on the carpet when she was standing barefoot washing. Paraphernalia plays a great part in pleasure when it is accompanied by a lull of idleness. It was this lull that she ferociously missed in air travel. Plane journeys she regarded as a fortunately unique mixture of the frightening and the boring, outdoing even a stay in hospital. Air hostesses seemed uncompassionate creatures, scornful of fear and winsome in their giving of capricious names on the tannoy, their attention to businessmen travelling first-class, their ineptitude in placing small babies in Moses' baskets immediately under the screen of the in-flight film so that the flickering light caused a contagion of tired infant screaming. Climbing into bed after enjoyment of the drugget and the lighting arrangements, which were not bad at all considering the predicaments of British Rail, Lady Corfe gave mind to the old London North Eastern Railways, and at the same time, thinking being what it is, to plane fear. Her godfather, still alive, and a lifemanship practitioner of no mean art, had shared this among many other of her distastes. Once he had been traveling with her by plane to Paris, had felt her arms going rigid on the armrests even though he had given her the aisle seat in understanding of claustrophobia. He had said to her during the long-drawn-out takeoff, peering out of the window at the perpetual shambles of a then much younger London Airport, "I'm relieved to see we're using the north runway."

The old do not forget being young, any more than the young forget being old, she thought. Now, there's a curious

40

truth; but if one ever needed amateur proof that Einstein was right about relativity, it's sitting in the nursery. Simon knows well what it's like to be my age.

Lady Corfe, now best called Averil, troubled about Tony's life. At Simon's age he had already been world-weary, as though all experience were found dulled and wanting. Something overproficient about the way he treated people, even when he was only ten. What a way to think of him. If she had been in less hospitable circumstances than this train, if she had been another woman, she would have wept. It had possibly been her fault for sending him to boarding school. It had seemed the right thing, for an only child in the wilds of their big house, but Harrow had put him into an age ghetto instead of living a life in common with the gardener, the organist at Hexham Abbey, her husband and herself, two teenage friends in the nearest village. The loss seemed to have made him vow never again to engage in friendship. Eliza had never been a friend of his; at best an adversary, at worst a commodity. In place of intimates it seemed that he had sworn to himself to have only craven secretaries, court cuckolds, and those well-dined amusers who can be trusted never to lapse into the peril of judgment. It would be because of this, she thought, that he so disliked Mickey, dislike being the frequent mask of fear on those committed to the implacabilities of worldliness. Eliza's young and only lover, Dick, most loyal: Dick constituted no such danger. Averil often pondered and regretted the strange absence of sexual jealousy or ordinary fear in her son. Fear was something she could always scent as the precedent of anger, because she knew it very well herself. In others she could smell its onset as an epileptic has a potent warning smell of something like acetone before an attack. Tony, while she was on this journey, in this bunk voyaging back to the family's homeland, seemed to her some sort of mutant. And then again, a solitary boy looking

41

after his rabbits, deeply interested at the age of six by the way Beatrix Potter expressed "the soporific effect of lettuce," now grown bitter by the sense of absurdity in loneliness that can plague the small despot. It seemed to her that he was in danger of giving up even the grown-up tasks that were no more than his assiduity in asking from school for news of his rabbits. He was surrounded in his profession by much to be done; every possible knowledge of bureaucracy's and politics' disaffection was available to him: but he bent his mania for activity to side-long matters. If one can't mend the public, he now seemed to her to think, one had better mend old shoes. His cynicism bit hard.

Averil lay awake all night, reading and thinking. She was accustomed anyway to being awake for the sight of the sparks shooting up from the steel works at Consett in County Durham, now closed down. Unemployment here was the worst in England. The absence of the steel works flung her still further into wakefulness, as absences will. She got dressed, through long habit of beating insomnia by being disobliging to it, and went along the train corridor to see if anyone could get her an early cup of coffee. The sleeping-car attendant was in his cubbyhole playing with a Rubik cube.

"I'll brew it up, madam. You'll be getting the top of the crop. They give us instant now, to my disgust, but it's the lingering in the old steel urns that wrecks it. Coffee boiled is coffee spoiled."

She inspected his Rubik cube. "This is the four-way one. I can't begin."

"It's a measure of me, in the night especially. The three-brick one is a knockdown."

"I can't do even that. My grandson has one and he's always telling me not to mess it up and then twisting it and getting it right again in under a minute. He clocks himself. I don't think he really minds sorting out what I've done. Otherwise it's like playing noughts and crosses with himself."

The train attendant was sitting opposite her with an eye on the kettle. A small white-faced man with a nose like a paw.

"More like playing chess with himself. Interesting what even a boy will set himself. From what you say, he'd not be into double figures yet?"

"Getting on."

"Aye, then, he's already at it."

"I'd noticed that they'd shut down Consett. I knew, but it's strange not to see the sparks."

"Grass on the shipyards, like the thirties. It's the thirties all over again."

"You wouldn't have been born."

"You don't have to have been born to remember things, do you." He made the coffee. "I daresay you like it black. There's some brown sugar if you care for it."

"A choice between sugars on British Rail?"

"It's my own. I keep it with my snap." He got his lunch box. "The wife keeps the supply going for me. Last time she filled it, a bomb squad opened it. There's not much harm an explosive detector can do to brown sugar and a sardine sandwich."

He stopped her from using too little sugar, saying that brown sugar was strengthening in the nighttime, though the dawn was nearly up now.

"Brown sugar to white is like honey in the comb to honey in a jar." His voice was the true voice of the North-East, distinct and particular, not flattened out by television. Averil had thought herself at home already when she heard it at King's Cross, and now she could hear it under the surface of her own voice.

"Was your father on the railways?" she said, after inspecting his Rubik cube without messing it up.

"No, he was the gardener to Mr. Trevelyan. You'll have heard of him. He lived at Wallington. Ten miles to the west of Morpeth."

43

"The great-nephew of Macaulay."

"Mr. Trevelyan wrote history books himself. I didn't follow his writing but he worked like the devil and he also walked like the devil. He used to say his two legs were his two doctors. Mr. Ruskin and Mr. Swinburne often used to come to Wallington in Mr. Macaulay's day, but that's the extent of my knowledge of him as a writer."

"You father would have had many a story."

"He was quite a young man when he died, so I didn't hear much. I could tell you more about Mr. Trevelyan's taste in roses. Or we could talk about Robert Surtees. A great study, Mr. Surtees. I believe they're too busy with punk and jogging in some places to have heard of him. I get all the punk and jogging news on the radio, such as it amounts to."

"You've got enough time for Surtees."

"There's always time if you've got a job. That is, if you're lucky enough to have a job."

"You've got enough to do. Everyone to wake up."

"There's only you and me in this carriage. There's the great British Rail for you. People seem to have lost the taste for trains. It's always a pity to see anything passing."

"Surtees. I never thought to meet a man at dawn who could tell me about him."

"I spent two months in service at the library when I scarpered from school. The pay was welcome. Of Mr. Surtees I couldn't speak much, but as a matter of his literary powers I always took to him. Took to him as a personage. He liked his claret mulled. A rumbustious friend, he'd have been, with his hunting over hedges the height of Hadrian's Wall. Always first at the meet, he'd have been."

Time passed intimately in the wagon-restaurant attendant's little quarters. They were enclosed in the darkness that makes talk spasmodic and open. Ruminative moments over the Rubik cube, the people long dead whom they knew of as well as the living. As the dawn came up, the everyday began to take over. Tea to be got. Talk of Surtees and Swinburne and Macaulay prompted a sudden direct question from Averil: "Do you happen to know Braw Fell?"

"My grandfather's best friend was the agent."

"My grandfather was Sir Douglass."

The usual Northumbrian silence while the attendant filled up the tea urn. "Then you'd be Miss Tess's granddaughter. We heard a lot about her. I never had the honour."

"You wouldn't have been born."

"She was forcibly fed to get the vote for women. My father on the railways knew about her from his father. Sir Douglass went to prison with her on two long occasions and was forcibly fed himself. It made him the mockery of men in the South."

"He was condescending to women in the beginning."

"A miracle hand at inventions. He could change the weather."

"Did you hear much talk of my grandmother?"

"Well, she was famous, wasn't she? The forcible feeding affected her throat and she fell to every disease that was going. Her sister died of the same thing. Strong as rivets they were, but it was asking too much. They say the papers they inherited, documents, were too much for them. And then I don't have knowledge."

"I inherited the papers. Mostly from women in prison."

"A subject of mortal concern." The attendant looked out at the daylight. "So you'd be Miss Averil. Well, I daresay this train has seen you before." He took a swig of boiling water and said, "I find it's good for the bronchials. Waste of time, doctors. Come back if it doesn't get better, they say. Well, you wouldn't have gone in the first place if it had, would you." He offered her a mug of the drink and she sipped it.

45

"It's improved with a drop of lemon squash."

"You've been to Braw Fell?" said Averil.

"Your mother was trying to turn the red rhododendrons blue."

"I haven't been for a while. What color are they now?"

"Blue. A success. But there's need of a dose of iron, I hear."

A while later, as they were pulling into Newcastle, Averil gave the man a pound note in an envelope. He helped her down with her luggage, having changed from his white jacket back into Railway uniform, and waved to a woman in jeans and a short thick overcoat at the barrier.

"That's my wife," he said. "Usually she gets here after me, but there's plenty of transport this time of the morning and she must have gott'n the sooner bus."

For some reason the sight of Newcastle Railway Station brought back to Averil a story that her mother had told, of a suffragette friend known as La Belle Maloney who followed the young Churchill about and at Bristol Railway Station menaced him with a dog whip, crying, "Take that, in the name of the insulted women of England!" Averil's mother was called Tess Radlett. Decades ago she had written at the height of the suffragette movement, "The campaign is our Eton and Oxford, our regiment, our ship."

3

elying its name, Braw Fell lies rather high, though indeed surrounded by the brown-looking burns—becks—of Northumberland. The burns look brown because, crystal though the water is, it flows over pebbles and rocks that obstinately remain brown as if to be stubborn to the whims of cavalier self-good-wishers plunging their arms into the burn so as to produce a white pebble and the opportunity to make a wish. Wishes are not so glibly made in Northumberland nor sanctity so easily given. Safe conduct to any Northumbrian will mean touching the frith stool of Hexham Abbey.

In Northumberland at the turn of the century Averil's mother, Tess, wrote, "To allow us all to start from one point in the world of intellectual culture and labour, with one Ancient Mother Nature sitting as umpire, distributing the prices and scratching from the lists the incompetent, is all we demand. Throw the puppy into the water: if it swims, well; if it sinks, well; but do not tie a rope round its throat and weight it with a brick and then assert its incapacity to float."

Tess lived with her newly married husband, owner of an estate where the Victorian wealth was coming in from shipbuilding, in conditions of emancipation that hovered still on the brink of enforced timidity. Like Jane Austen before her as she wrote her novels, Tess hid the part of the manifesto she had been writing under her letters when her husband, Douglass, came into the room and pretended to have been continuing her endless correspondence with her nephews and nieces in other parts of the country.

"The hydraulic phaeton is working," said Douglass. "Mr. Carlisle has just taken me for a ride to the rhododendron walks in it."

Tess fell into a moment of thought about the rhododendrons. They were red and she was determined to make them blue. She had read somewhere in a volume of the *Boy's Encyclopedia of Knowledge* that iron in the soil turned red bushes a delicate shade of blue. So by night she had been turfing up the soil with the household brass shovel and patiently inserting rations of iron from a heavy bag of iron dust that she had sent for by mail order these days. The sending of the money had presented difficulties because she had no chequebook, but she saved up the money from the housekeeping allowance that her husband gave her and had the iron sent to the cook, a trusted friend. Tess's preference for blue rhododendrons to red reflected nothing dangerously political. It was simply that she had read that soldiers wounded in the Crimea had found blue a more soothing color than hospital green, and she thought that men these days could do with soothing, like women.

Her husband stood in front of the fire. He remarked irritably on the presence of soil on the coal shovel, which he said should be investigated by her with the housemaid. He read to her from *The Times*: from an editorial that he mistakenly thought she would not read for herself later. It described the suffragettes as "the hysterical, the neurotic, the idle, and the habitual imbibers of excitement."

"Dear Douglass," said Tess, "it makes them, or us, sound

48

like drunkards in a lunatic asylum doing petit point for charity beggars."

"Yes, my darling. It goes on. Some of them are out with their hammers because of dreary, empty lives and overexcitable natures. They are regrettable products of our civilization. The article continues with a very powerul letter from Sir Almott Wright, a physician. He believes that militancy is the result of mental illness. Nearly fifty percent of women go slightly crazy in middle life and are therefore liable to become frantic. The mind of a woman, he holds, is always threatened with danger from the reverberation of her physiological experiences and it is with such thoughts that the doctor lets his eyes rest on the militant suffragist."

"One day it will be *her* eyes."

"I beg your pardon? I was reading on to myself."

"One day there will be plenty of women physicians."

"To go on, he makes the point that there are no good women, only women who have lived under the influence of good men."

"And one day the reverse will be true too, except that it seems to my mind, if you forgive the reference, a cruel point of view for any physician. Or indeed anyone at all. Even our Labrador has his own character, nothing to do with yourself or me or Hilda."

Hilda was the cook, whose company the Labrador liked.

"In any case, to go on again, the eminent physician sees them as being two kinds of militant. The sexually embittered, whose legislative programme is licence for themselves or else restriction for men, and the incomplete, whose programme is to convert the world into an epicene institution in which men and women shall everywhere work side by side at the selfsame tasks for the selfsame pay."

"Do you agree?"

49

"They are his words, but the sentiments have the bell-ring of truth. He goes on in his conclusion to say that 'Even in animals—I say "even," because even in these at least one of the sexes has periods of complete quiescence—male and female cannot be safely worked side by side unless they are incomplete.' I must say, my love, that as I read him *verbatim* he sounds a little redoubtable, but that's the order of *The Times* and the majesty of the medical profession itself. You look a little mopey. Give up your letter-writing and let me take you for a healing jaunt in the wondrous mechanized phaeton."

In the phaeton, which proceeded jumpily, but which he handed her into as if into a royal carriage, he said to Tess with more comprehension than his words carried, "I have to tell you, Tess, that there are grave political consequences that could follow if the militants are irresponsible. I am not including you, for I count you a rational being. But the Kaiser is said to be depending on the support of the suffragettes against the British government they have done so much to shake and discredit."

They passed the rhododendron patch.

"Our Labrador is hunting for a bone, it seems. You will speak to Hilda about it and ask her to see that things are mended. I can see that you are still not yourself. I daresay the voice of *The Times* upset you. A man forgets the frailty of the sex he loves and tends. We shall go on with our ride as far as the lake. The shudder of excitement in this machine is the very shudder of progress itself. Lean over and take the wheel and you will feel it, my dear one." He handed her the wheel and went on, "Miss Pankhurst insists that what Germany wants is victory for British pacifists under the leadership of either Mr. Asquith or what she calls Mr. Bolshevik Henderson. She wants all our prewar books on economics and labour questions to be publicly burned because she says they are so full of right-wing or left-wing prejudices. Now, that can't be right either, can it? It leaves very little room for lack of prejudice."

"I don't think she's a patch on her mother," Tess said. "Why did you say 'prewar'?"

"Because I feel sure, and feel sure of course also from what you say, that war is coming sooner or later."

Not falling prey to the feminine quiescence foreseen by Douglass, Tess carried on in wartime with dual force. She helped to found a forebear of a Working Woman's College in Newcastle, aided by the earlier act of the Christian Socialists in the South—Charles Kingsley, Frederick Denison Maurice—in their conception in 1848 of Queen's College. Queen's had been established by men to educate the governesses employed by the rich to tutor girl children in all that governesses then knew: drawing, a little French, reading, etiquette, and music. The subject of music led often to the learning of the harp in the case of the otherwise hopelessly unmarriageable plain daughters who were blessed at least with becoming elbows. Tess bought books on mathematics and calculus and medicine under the cover of her husband's accounts at Durham bookshops. She even bought textbooks in advance for her children, Averil and Lily, building up a library almost as soon as they were born. The acceptance of one of her club's students as the first woman anaesthetist gave her a keen sense of accomplishment. She became more and more involved in the suffragists' movement, which often took her South.

Averil as a girl had a day with the decorous man who was the Rector of the Abbey. She loved Hexham, capital of Hexham-shire, which is the heart of Northumberland's extraordinary history. The Abbey in turn, going back to the twelfth century, is the centre of what people come to think of as both the religious source and the marketplace of their shire. In the twelfth century the Abbey was the Hall of Pleas for the archbishops.

51

Hexhamshire was then an early regality separate from the rest of England. In the Abbey, Averil had finished her lesson with the organist, who fascinated her not only with his foot dexterity but also with his ears, which had hair growing out of them that made them look to her like gooseberries. It was one of the two things about her Hexham that made this waif-looking, white-faced child collapse into giggles. The other was that, in the face of struggle under such people as—no one can help their names—King Wilfrid and Queen Ethelrid of Northumbria, it had been burned along with the rest of Tyneside by the self-evidently savage Halfdene the Dane. No doubt a heretical monster, but a Halfdene the Dane gives the Dark Ages a bad name.

The Rector of the Abbey was kneeling at the altar in his white robe, alone, without a congregation, sipping from a goblet. After a while he turned round and came back to Averil, sitting far back on an uncomfortable chair.

"I didn't realize you were here," he said.

"You were practising," she said.

He showed her the frith stool again, to get over her fear of it. It was in a Saxon crypt much older even than the rest of the Abbey. The crypt was roofed with big and very North Country–looking stones, backed and carved and often inscribed by the Roman invaders who had worked their way North in their chilly attempt to possess Britain. Averil was still terrified by the darkness of the place, and the Rector tried to humanize it for her in his own manner.

"The closer you could get to the frith stool, the safer you were. If you could get near enough to lay your hands on it you were entirely safe." It was a nightmare, alive in the daylight after her music lesson, and ever afterward Averil had a matching fear of cellars. Seeing her panic about damp places underground—which placed in Averil her first mistrust of sophistry

52

in mustiness, of mutterings to confessional boxes cloaked in heavy velvet, of childhood games involving hiding in places called sanctuary that turned out to be crabbed grown-ups' superstitions readily despoiled with a yell by carelessly hostile children or adults of ill-disposition—seeing her panic, the Rector took her up to the north aisle.

"I particularly like these carvings," he said, talking in detail because he knew her.

"The bottom part shows us St. George; a fox, dressed as a monk preaching to very Hexham-looking men playing musical instruments; a lady doing her hair; and a monkey eating a lot of buns. And then look at this hallowed rogue. He's listening to prayer, I thought at first. No, of course, he's stealing a sheep. The cattle raids and sheep raids across the border went on until longer than one might think."

"Fred the shepherd lost half his lambs and it wasn't the snow because there weren't any bodies and the mother sheep would have found them if he hadn't. He's a good looker for things and he didn't lose a mother sheep, because they're good lookers too; so it must have been the Scots over the Wall."

"I wouldn't put it down to the Scots. I like these carvings." The figures were squat, with squared faces and hunched shoulders; pagan, local, respectful. The Rector took Averil away to a stairway.

"Hundreds of years ago, choirboys used to process singing down this stairway. They often got soaked and their pleated linen collars looked like wet paper darts. Well, anyway, down this stairway came the choirboys, and no one could understand the drenching until someone realized the marauding Scots had burned the roof open and rain dripped onto the bottom stairs and the choirboys were in a cascade. It wasn't always pouring rain, it was often an ancient building's drip. A present-day architect would have detected it in a second, not being able to charge for professional slowness. But they kept shut up about it because with Gregorian chants going on they got a huge amount of pleasure from getting soaked. That would be very indicative of what's called the Hexham measure."

"It's that much bigger than any other market measure in the land."

"Well, it would be, given Hexham."

She looked askance at such profligacy.

The Rector had often asked her if she preferred him in vestments or with a tie. She said either, being bossed about as she was about clothes herself. Her adored younger sister had been born three years after Averil and it seemed that she had been produced to grow into Averil's clothes (put away in scented linen cupboards—the only warm place in this refrigerator of a grange) for merely such a purpose and no more. The factory, on the other hand, was blessedly warm. The Rector (in his vestments) and his wife gave her haggerty and roast beef and two vegetables, with gravy out of a Georgian sauceboat.

"Mamma's away. Papa says she's not very well. What's the matter with her? Is she in hospital?"

"Not exactly."

"Is she in prison?"

Silence.

"Why?" said Averil.

"Women's rights. Or theft of men's misrights, you could say."

"Do you want some more haggerty?" said the Rector's wife. Averil was helped to more of the Northumbrian recooked and seasoned and sliced potatoes with meat-dripping to brown them.

"As to the word 'theft,' I didn't use it understandably just now," said the Rector. "But women like your mother have put themselves into a difficult position down South." The Rector had some more roast meat and cauliflower and carrots and hag-gerty from his wife, cut again into the Yorkshire pudding (cooked in a big square tin under the beef dripping, and still high at the edges and in patches in the resplendent browned middle of batter-risen bog), and said, "Your mother's fighting for a Hexham measure, that one, and so will you be, I don't doubt."

"And Lily, though she's younger."

"And Lily indeed. I remember she didn't cry at the appointed time at her christening, an omission which is stupidly said to be unlucky. Only because all less staunch-witted babies do it."

"She doesn't like the name Mamma and Papa gave her."

"That could always be changed," said the Rector.

"Not without another christening, and she's too old for that. She's nearly six. I call her something else anyway so it doesn't matter because she doesn't speak to other people. I showed her that nun's book you gave me two weeks ago, the one called *I Chose Silence,* and she agreed."

"I didn't know she read," said the Rector.

"Oh, yes. She read when she was four, as soon as I could teach her. The thing about reading is not to let on, like having a rabbit hutch which is a great consolation as long as nobody knows about it."

Moving on to apple snow, the Rector looked at his wife in some predicament about what to do.

"We'll shift back to theft," he said, clearing his throat in front of this difficult congregation that singularly possessed the authority of Averil's steadfast politeness and of her greater youth.

"As I said, it was entirely misleading to apply the word to women's rights. We will get further if we think of Hexham. Apple snow? Or there's apple crumble left over if you'd rather. And cream."

"Apple snow and no cream, thank you, please."

"I thought you liked cream. From our own Hexham cows."

"The cream keeps being vegetablish these days. Our gardener says the cows have been at the turnips. The milk is worse. I've gone off cows because they've gone off us, our gardener says. Which is worse, swedes or turnips or parsnips or Jerusalem artichokes?"

"Swedes," said the Rector bravely. Decision was the mark of his career.

"As to theft, because leaving a started topic unexplained is like leaving around one of a pair of dirty socks, and oh dear I don't like the connection with swedes, now I've quite gone off all root vegetables including even carrots—in any case, hauling ourselves limply back to the case of the theft, the idea of theft, which was where we went off the trail, what I wanted to say was that market day in Hexham used to be one hell of a day. Excuse me while I read at table, my dear," he said to his wife, and winking at Averil through one glass of his spectacles, which he was starting to put on in readiness to read from the pile of books that he always had at his plateside and that no one was allowed to touch. From a cracked old leather volume with a flapping spine.

"We read that 'in Exhamm itself every Markatt day ther is eighty or one hundred strong thieffes and the pore men and gentilmen also seethe them whiche didd robbe them and their goodys and dare nother complayne of them by name nor say oone word to them.'"

The Rector took off his spectacles and went on.

"'One can see them shopping in crowds beside the shambles...'" To Averil: "That being the old name for the board for cutting up animals."

"Not just after roast beef, dear," said his wife.

"Averil has the stomach for such things if needed, like her mother. One can see the shoppers and the thieves, 'thieffes,' among the Hexham glovemakers, with their usual thin big-boned Northern faces like Averil's here, who has never looked to me like a child."

The Rector's wife said fast, gently, "Are you worried about your mother?"

"She's fine. I'm not a child."

The Rector and his wife kept helplessly talking about food, though it was soft comfort.

"We'll make some gooseberry fool for you to take home. I've got some cream that couldn't possibly make you think of swedes."

"Normally I would love to make gooseberry fool, but today it would be like eating my teacher's ears."

The Rector's wife said, "Does your teacher grow gooseberries? Which teacher?"

"The Hexham Abbey organist. He grows gooseberry hairs in his ears. It's better than Buxtehude, but Bach takes my mind off them. The hairs. I quite like them. I haven't said anything to him, and he knows I'm keen on his feet too, especially when he's playing Bach."

"His favourite piece in the Abbey is the painting of the Virgin Mary near the high altar."

"Is it yours?"

"Her mixture of holiness and unholy sardonic humour," said the Rector. "I like that. And being interested in missionary work abroad after all our time in Kenya and the Gold Coast, I find my attention very much taken by the man being trampled by an apparently triumphant horse. Did you notice him?"

"Of course," said Averil, whose eye had immediately caught the victim of what seemed at others' glance to be a piece of emblematic iconography: man prone, rider on horse rampant.

"The man who is being trampled has a pike that he is going to stick into the horse," said Averil.

"It makes me think of Africa. You think you've alleviated

the difficulties of Africa and then you see you haven't and then it's making its own way and defending itself for all it's worth. Africans would make very good Northumbrians."

"Could I have some more apple snow? Why haven't we got Africans here?"

The Rector's wife said, "The trouble is, they'd almost inevitably be asked as servants."

"Mamma doesn't believe in servants."

The Rector looked pompous for the first time, ringing the deep bell tone of his voice as if he were announcing his own sermon.

"Nothing unctuous about Braw Fell. There is a great difference between giving service and being slavish. We are growing too nervous of the simple word 'feudalism.' Landowner and villein worked together in soothed harmony." Seeing possibilities in his thought, he made a note of what he had said with a little gold pen on a pad that his wife laid out for him at every mealtime.

4

*T*here was indeed, as the Rector said, nothing unctuous about Braw Fell, the monument to late-Victorian belief in the pefectibility of man that had been built by Douglass Borthwick, Averil's father. Sir Douglass had been born in Gosforth, Newcastle, of a poorish family. Once he had made his fortune he bought fourteen thousand acres of land near Hexham and came there to build Braw Fell. No absentee builder he. Sir Douglass, knighted for his services to shipbuilding, was a gentle fanatic who broke the rules. Braw Fell was an extraordinary monument that mixed the notions of castle, manse, and electrical workshop. What he first envisaged as a fortress developed into a pleasure palace. He was very much a man of his place. Within Braw Fell, he seemed to be in a world of arrow-slit Northumbrian castles gorged on Victorian aspirations to Xanadu. Hydraulic gongs invented by Sir Douglass as a sideline for his immense energy would ring for meals. He produced hydraulic lifts. The Prince of Wales had been sufficiently impressed by his diligence during that last century of belief in the natural drift of the invincibility of *homo sapiens* to come to stay at Braw Fell for the trout fishing. Douglass himself was not much interested in nature, though he could be incited by it when he saw it as convertible. It was in the changeable that he rejoiced, and things could more readily be bent to change by theory than the intransigent countryside he had grown up in. It was theory that would melt the world and re-create it in the image of men's ideas. A hydraulic engine re-volving the water mechanisms in the conservatory bespoke the triumph of invention; the orchids it was watching did not. Though a natural churchgoer, Sir Douglass placed no great stock in the achievements of the Almighty over the work of Creation. More had to be done, much more. Here Tess and Douglass were in clear accord. And man was here to do it: "the term 'man' embracing women, as Mary Baker Eddy puts it," his wife would say tartly. There seemed no end to the activity at Braw Fell. It was the first house in England to be lit by electric-ity. Sir Douglass, no great music lover but tireless in pursuit of mechanisms that would bring the new to the ear, had an Aeo-lian-mode pianola attached to a Bechstein. An unusual sound was made. He was also intent on doing away with the idea of the well-tempered scale: he had studied the theory of musical overtones that had led Bach to write *The Well-Tempered Clavier*, and felt that it was in need of reinspection. This was one of the many projects that occupied his spare time in the middle of the night. Papers to do with the innovative, projects in progress, littered his dressing room like muddy hunting boots pulled off by men in a hurry. One of his other schemes was to investigate a special binding for books to be printed on artificial paper that would be a quarter of the weight of the changed timber that tired out his arms when he was reading above his head in bed at night. Artificial-paper samples, exqui-sitely metered hydraulic scales, and tight coils of possible wire bindings were everywhere.

Another scheme was to make a sixteen-hour Kino film about Leonardo da Vinci. Sir Douglass admired Leonardo above any-one else, and he possessed a drawn copy of the da Vinci note-books pirated by a soulmate of infallible memory on a long art-gallery foray. The attempt at the flying machine had moved him to tears once more when he had the third of three sleepless nights in a row during a union crisis at the shipyard. When the Shah of Persia came to stay, there was quarter-tone untempered music piped into the dining room at dinnertime. Several small plates of carefully differentiated pickles were served to the Shah in the painstaking belief that they would make him feel at home. The dining room, originally papered in beautiful flocked wallpaper, was painted over because of Sir Douglass's thought, based on careful scientific theory, that wallpaper glue gives off noxious fumes. This concern passed on to the Shah, who was held in a vise grip of interest by Braw Fell. Braw Fell was mock-everything: mock-Saxon, mock-Tudor, mock-Wagnerian, even mock-Northumbrian and mock-Chelsea. It was full of gables and huge fireplaces. In the library there was stained glass by William Morris.

The finished motley house, a very craggy pleasure dome, was a thrumming factory of the new and the purposeful, run on feudal but sharply striving lines. The maids got up at half-past six and had half a day off a week, plus every other Sunday. The gardeners emulated Sir Douglass in pushing ahead of the natural course of the year by two seasons through weather conditions excitingly created in huge greenhouses, including snow in June and an improbable heathery heat wave in January. The Shah had been enthralled to find fog at his beck and call in May, having thought it limited to November.

"We are pushing Nature on at twice the usual rate," said Sir Douglass. "For Nature without the aid of man is doomed. There will be a world food crisis unless man steps in. I find that some of the most interested subscribers to my pamphlet on the topic are women. I had one visit last week at my office by a charming mother of six who asked whether it was possible for man's intelligence to speed up pregnancy. It *must* be possible." The Shah, in profound disagreement, assented to the line of argument. Even for a Shah, hard social tasks were set him. This speeding-up-of-Nature job, for one. Acquiescence in such an endeavour belied the family ethics of generations. It struck him that he had not responded genially enough, so he interpolated that he had no doubt that Her Majesty Queen Victoria in her heyday of fertility would have been the first to welcome such an idea. And another test: the bread-making. It was done naked in the morning by the head cook, Hilda Lauderdale. Like Elsie down South years later, she did it in bulk every day for the whole household, plaiting it, leaving it to rise, cooking it in the bread ovens at the left of the kitchen range. She had done the job naked all her working life, simply finding it easier to have to wash the flour only off herself and not off her cook's uniform, and also less hot. The maids were perfectly used to the sight and went about their business. The undergardener waited until seven to come in with the vegetables for the day and to take the next day's order for the kitchen garden after a cup of tea, by which time the cook—Hilda—was unfloured, dressed, and having her own cup of black Continental coffee, which she preferred to tea.

It being April and still chilly, Averil joined the kitchen soon after lunching with the vicar and had a cupful of peptonized chocolate, made with water because of the dislike of milk. It was brewed from a tinful of syrupy chocolate base sold as a health food by John Bell and Croyden in London and sent by the dozen on to Braw Fell. Averil's and an undergardener's right index fingers (the undergardener being fourteen) were perpetually bloodied or faintly healing from scraping the remnants of the chocolate jam from the inside of a discarded tin opened, not with Sir Douglass's hydraulic tin opener, but with an old-fashioned opener that left jagged edges. Her father's opener looked to Averil like a surgical hacksaw as people in the kitchen talked.

"I went to Newcastle last Saturday to the club and there was a sketch onstage about this doctor. This barber-surgeon," said an undergardener, waxing descriptive, "he rushed onstage. It was Cromwell's time; place littered with poultry and geese and parasols abandoned and lives petering out; legs kicking everywhere in need of his ready hacksaw; everywhere in the midst of all these feathers; and first thing he does is go over to the only dead body in the carnage, covered with a sheet, obviously a dead 'un, and lift back the sheet with his hacksaw at shoulder level, swift in action, and say sympathetically, 'We *are* in a bad way, aren't we?'" Most of the kitchen laughed. Hilda stirred her black coffee. Averil said, "I don't see what's funny about that."

"It's funny because of the feathers," said an underhousemaid. "Every time we have someone new to stay, there's a new storm of feathers because Sir will insist on Northumberland feathers and making your own pillows. Myself, I'd just as soon they came from Durham if they stick together better. These here just don't hold up and I don't fancy going to Newcastle to see feathers even if I were asked."

"No, it's funny because of all the people in real need of the hacksaw who are being neglected," said Hilda.

Averil screamed into a kitchen cushion and put her fingers into her ears.

"Have a plait of bread, hinny," said Hilda, removing one of the fingers in Averil's ears. "With peptonized chocolate. There's a tin I was going to throw away, and I daresay you could find a lot in it." Pause. "You always do find a lot in things. You're the image of your father, young Averil."

This was what Hilda called her: "young Averil," as though she had had older Averil predecessors, as indeed she had a hundred and fifty years ago.

"Put on your rabbit coat. You were always a starvesome mortal," said Hilda, seeing her through the back door with the land agent, Frederick Carlisle. Mr. Carlisle talked by gender about his flowers. Usually they tended to be "she." Trees were always "he." "He's coming along fine, this little Canadian maple, among all these benighted English oaks grown from the acorn. I don't know how Sir does it," Mr. Carlisle said to Averil in one of the whirring off-season greenhouses. He put on an extra sweater. "It may be April out there but it's still only February in this particular greenhouse."

Mr. Carlisle took Averil into another greenhouse to show her some Christmas roses.

"Bye, lovely, you see, nobody's watching them when I bring them into the house because people don't know the miracle of it. Christmas roses in April. The Shah himself didn't know the miracle. But as he's foreign, his seasons would be different and I daresay his mind is on other matters."

"He gave me something called a caftan. It scratches my neck. It's pretty, though I don't know when Lily or me could wear it because it's yards taller than we are, even if we're piled on top of each other, which we quite often are. As, for instance, confidentially, when we play the sextopus."

"Anything to do with sex?"

" 'Sex' meaning 'six' in Latin. She puts her legs around my waist and I go onto the ground with my hands and she crawls between my legs on her arms and then we move on six legs. It only works because of the difference between her age and mine. It won't be possible for very long more. Nothing ever is." Averil gave the heavy sigh of children which always sounds hounded by intimations of instant immortality beyond the bounds of grown-up foresight. The fate of a benighted world that dreamed itself to be ceaseless was on her shoulders.

The Shah, a kindly-seeming despot, took her onto his lap at some point and told her a story that had been told him by his father's driver about Queen Victoria's driver. His own father's driver had sped him around and ahead of the traffic, with, it seemed, some adroitness, at the turning to Buckingham Palace by Marlborough House. Queen Victoria's driver had leaned out of the window of her less overbearing gig and said to a policeman directing the traffic, a man to whom he had been taught to be obedient, "Who does he think he is, the Shah of Persia?"

"Yes," said the policeman, beckoning the Queen's car forward. "I've been taught to keep our place," shouted the English royal driver, patronized in a traffic jam. "We don't take advantage."

"The point of that," said the Shah, "the comic part is about actually being the Shah of Persia, and the serious part is about Queen Victoria's driver behaving better."

"I see the comic part," said Averil. "But somebody's got to be really the Shah of Persia after all, like you, and you'd expect the policeman to know that. The serious part isn't right. A driver is supposed to get a Shah or anyone to where he wants to get to fast. Papa has often driven me, and he drives like the wind but you couldn't call it rude of him, he's just being helpful if he has to drop me for my organ lesson on the way back to the shipyards."

"That would be too early for your organ lesson because he told me he's in at the yards by half-past six."

"The organist is an early riser and I use the gap to do harmony and counterpoint and practise blasted thirds."

"What does 'blasted' mean?"

"Same as 'bloody,' but I'm not allowed to say 'bloody' for another year. It's like being allowed to make a pudding of your meat and vegetables and potatoes. It means mashing them all together. I'm not allowed to do that after my next birthday."

Again the heavy sigh of childhood.

"You can't win 'em all," she said.

"Where did you hear that?"

"When we were talking about Blaydon races. I could play that to you on the organ, but it's better with a lot of people singing it. They sing it in the shipyards. A man called Joseph Price has just done a demonstration. We all saw it. In the first three miles the tide was against him when he was towing his sailship; the first time a sailing ship had ever been towed by a steamboat."

"How do you know about it?"

"I've studied rigging and so on."

And so it came about that the Shah of Persia and Averil and her younger and silent sister Lily went by the hydraulic phaeton to the shipyards in Newcastle. Frederick Carlisle, who had worked at Alnwick Castle before Braw Fell, came with them to order some spare parts and Portuguese tiles and electric flex for the estate. It was the Portuguese tiling that was most on his mind. It was needed for the floor of a hydraulic fountain installation that was to move the wines and Madeira and port at Sir Douglass's side in the dining room. The dining room seemed to be outside—pine trees and magnolia and seedling grass flourishing around the sideboard—though it was fully heated against the Northumbrian snows and protected by triple glazing with floodlights onto pine trees. What the agent wanted was white tiling, snow white, to cover not only the floor but also the walls, with the green shapes of the pine trees outside drawn in a perspective so that there was no apparent right angle between floor and wall. There would be moonlight, from a special lighting fixture to follow the courses of the moon. He and Sir Douglass had worked it all out with the help of books on the Medicis about false perspective, which they, of course, had been able to improve on, given the superior knowledge of any man born in the nineteenth century. He could see

66

it all. He and Sir Douglass worked as a team. He took the Shah and Averil and Lily, the sisters in their sailor suits, to the yards.

"Ah," the Shah said, apparently agape with the wonder of the wheel-springing in the hydraulic phaeton, though overwhelmed by the dragon gasps of the mechanisms. "Now tell me about Braw Fell, if you please."

"Braw Fell's a world," said Carlisle on the way to Newcastle. "I used to be a shipping engineer in Sunderland and I thought I'd miss the sea, but of course we're only eight miles here from the North Sea. Within about a hundred miles' radius I've found everything to keep a man interested. I come from the part of Northumberland that sticks into Scotland like a thumb. Alnwick's there. We've always been a sore thumb. Braw Fell is peaceful after a Sunderland shipbuilding yard—the tea schooners and so on . . ."

"Tea schooners, top mainsail, top foresail, bringing in the mainsheet," said Averil, bemused by sail. Lily was listening to her sister as usual. She saluted with her fingers correctly at the naval right angle to her forehead, and went on sorting the stones of the drive at Braw Fell, which she was clearing bit by bit. Self-assigned impossible tasks. The agent went on, ignoring Lily's stone-sorting.

"The place was so peaceful I couldn't think where to put myself. I wondered what I'd do. I used to wait for the noise to start. Well, under Sir Douglass and me we got Braw Fell going full steam. Apart from all the seafaring records I've got to keep up, and the architectural records, beautiful line drawings, I've got the room we call work-in-progress which of course is Sir Douglass's dressing room. We've soundproofed it with cork set four inches away from the wall, which gives a modern effect and allows all the noise we want. Such plans in there. One has to watch the chambermaid. We sent out to her for four bottles of green liquid just lately at three in the morning and she found a nice herbicide because we were making a colour test but she spread it around that we're murderers incarnate. Crouching around a zinc-lined gutter we'd made for laboratory tests. 'Sir Douglass lying in a gutter for want of a rich victim,' she said. She couldn't conceive of a daring experiment conducted with herbicide."

"No, standing in the gutter," said Averil, tapping Morse on the side of the phaeton. "Papa would never lie in the gutter."

"She's just invented the signal 'help' for people who are drowning," said Lily, loyal.

"I didn't invent it," said Averil. "It always existed, but people generally use SOS because an 'S' sound travels best across water. 'Help' is just as good and more understandable because nobody would say 'Hell' in these circumstances." They were nearing the coast, there having been many pauses. Frederick Carlisle said, out of nowhere, "I believe in committees. Braw Fell was always its own fair world. We even have our own gasworks. The men have meetings because if one man suffers every man suffers. The music rooms at Braw Fell, for instance. All the furniture covered up in plastic sheets, huge sheets of protective celloloid, as if we're in for a spring-clean, but the secret is we're converting the instruments to hydraulic pumping on the principle of the modern fire engine. That's one of many things about the modern side, this celluloid." The Shah remarked on the speed of the phaeton. Then Carlisle asked him about communications in Persia and the Shah politely passed the question back.

"Ah, there was a time in the early days, when Sir Douglass was reaching his prime in his knickerbockers and when Braw Fell was no more than a pile of stones that the North-East wind had blown on—he was living in a more-than-ordinary house even then—well, sir, even then we had twenty-two horses and if Sir had to get to London on business he'd be there to the split second. He knew there was better even than George Stephenson's train to come, and until he invented it he preferred horses, like his two daughters here. He'd just get on one horse and send others ahead and put up at posting houses and he'd be there. Well, the subject of communications is a fascinating study. Braw Fell is a very efficient world, always has been. We're fortunate in having so much stone. Look at the beauty of that rain on gravel. Even so near Newcastle I'll be bound that's our own gravel. Rain turns it purple, doesn't it? There's a stone room at Braw Fell where Miss Averil at the height of her seaman years used to practise being seasick by dangling bacon rind down her throat."

The Shah asked Averil if she wanted to be a seaman, seeing the impossibility of it, and she showed him knots with a piece of rope she had coiled in her sailor-suit pocket. She still insisted on a boy's sailor suit, not a girl's, and won, there being no obstacles from Tess, and certainly none from her father, who would always be in concert with anything novel that repudiated the innocuous. The Shah noticed that she had calluses on the balls of her palms and correctly admired them. She explained that she had for a long time been in the habit of rubbing her hands up and down the bark of trees to give them the look of a sailor's who had been shinning up ropes. She had pursued this discipline even longer than Lily in Lily's Augean effort to cleanse, sort, and replace the stones of Braw Fell's drive and paths. Sir Douglass knew about this labour, carried out daily by lugging around a toy wheelbarrow and using a garden hose, and perceived in it the beginnings of a fireman. Of all people, he was Averil's perfect and beloved mate, seeing no more bar to his daughter's aspirations than he would have done to his wife's running a shipbuilding yard.

* * *

The phaeton arrived at Sir Douglass's office in the shipyard and took the carriage-load around to the back, where Sir Douglass and his quail-shaped Miss Amy met them. The Shah was shown the launching ships, the steel-welding shops, the victuallers, the repair shops. They meant little to him. The daughters, swinging their legs in Miss Amy's office, knew this perfectly well.

"He needs to see some of the records," said Averil. "But it may be beyond him."

"He can read," Lily said unexpectedly.

"I think he's used to Arabic, or is it Persian? Miss Amy can tell him better. She can point out the cuttings. She's the keeper of the scrolls. Our scrolls."

Miss Amy stopped typing on her big brand-new Underwood and said to the Shah and Douglass as they came in, "How many days till the launching?"

"Thirty-nine if we pick up speed," said Sir Douglass excitedly, going into his office beyond to speak to someone in the yard.

"Miss Amy is going to tell you about Newcastle first," said Averil. The Shah sat down pleasantly, braced as guests must be.

"Well, sir, my grandfather remembers Newcastle in 1838 when the members for the British Association for the Advancement of Science came north for their eighth annual meeting. I've got a clipping here. It reads so, most accurate, 'The town had presented a gay and animated appearance during the whole of the week. Even during the period of holding the meetings of the several sections in the mornings, the principal thorough-fares were crowded; and when these were over, Grey Street, Grainger Street, and Blackett Street were almost impassable. Splendid equipages, drawn by noble and beautiful animals with gorgeous trappings, were to be seen whirling in various directions or waiting opposite the entrances to the several section rooms: in short, the splendour of the scene baffles description.

Mr. Grainger's new buildings have been a source of wonder and admiration to the thousands who have been led to visit Newcastle during the week.' And the *Newcastle Journal* says that 'Newcastle is a town which is making more studies in wealth, population, and importance than perhaps any other in the Empire.' "

"And the bit about the ball," said Averil.

Miss Amy read, forefinger pointing. " 'A splendid ball was given by the Mayoress on Monday evening in the Assembly Rooms, which were fitted up on a scale of great splendour expressly for the occasion. About half-past ten, the Mayor and Lady Ann Compton, daughter of the Marquis of Northampton, led off the ball to the tune of the "Keel Row." ' " Miss Amy pointed her dancing toe as she read. " 'Quadrilles, waltzes, and gallopades followed, and the dancing was continued with great spirit to a late hour.'

"We were still rural," said Miss Amy. "We always will be. It's still no more than a fraction of Northumberland that's industrial. But even then we had the coal, of course, and the steel, and Mr. Stephenson's railway. The scientists have been again twice, in 1863 and 1887. In the days of their first visit, shipbuilding was an old-fashioned business. The girls will have told you about Mr. Price and his towing. I can't get excited about it myself, but they do. They keep on telling me."

She pulled Averil's sailor suit into a shape that she felt was closer to a dress, and Averil wriggled away.

"Mamma got me this and she thinks it's nice," said Averil.

"Well," said Miss Amy, "I'm drawn into woman suffrage myself—who isn't here?—and I spent the first money I ever earned on my own typewriter to work on my shipbuilding treatise in the high hopes of getting a degree, as if we hadn't all got high hopes up here, but I still don't see anything against a proper skirt. I've been collecting copies of Miss Christabel Pankhurst's 'Home News' with the idea of getting them bound. There are lovely chronicles of suffrage receptions. 'Mrs. Pankhurst looked elegant in a trained evening gown,' it says here, and 'The Misses Pankhurst wore white dresses with worked yokes.' You see what I mean. And 'The refreshments were delicious, the strawberries and cream being especially so.' An eleven-year-old writes this about one gathering: 'Mrs. Pankhurst held an "At Home" at her beautiful house on May 28. There was a great number of people there. Dr. Pankhurst, as chairman, said in his speech that if the suffrage was not given to women, the results would be terrible. If a body was half of it bound, how was it to be expected that it would grow and develop properly. This body was the human race, and the fettered half, women. He then, with many compliments, called upon Mrs. Fenwick Miller to speak. Mrs. Fenwick Miller spoke of the attitude of the political leaders and the growing power of the Woman's Franchise League. Some opponents tried to prove that women were naturally inferior to men, but our girls won degrees and honours at the universities. Mrs. Pankhurst wore a black dress of grenadine with a train from the shoulders, and looked very handsome indeed.' " She moved herself back to her pile of press clippings and old dusty volumes marked by herself with pieces of neatly scissored paper.

The Shah had found the sailor-suit episode and its Pankhurst aftermath difficult to take, king that he was of a foundering country, and retreated gladly to the help of Miss Amy in telling what was, after all, a man's story. The buying of a private typewriter to work on a private endeavour was no cause for alarm. Since the invention of the typewriter—by, he felt to be axiomatic, a man—woman had sat behind it as obediently as behind a flatiron or a yashmak. The notion of independent use, such as Miss Amy's, did not occur.

"To understand England you have to understand the North-East. The sea is England's iron fence," said Miss Amy to the

Shah. "There's hardly a part of England where you can't hear seagulls. Never more than seventy-five miles from the sea. The first time the British Association met in Newcastle the members were delayed by everything going on. One of the people who most interested them was an Armstrong, William Armstrong, related to the young ladies here, who was trained as a solicitor. Hydraulics—" Then, turning, "No, Averil," who was fidgeting.

"Lily wants to go out for stones," said Averil. "The Shah's our duty, not stones." (Hushed voice to Miss Amy, keeper of much more than scrolls.) "He needs educating about women being able to go to sea. He could be a great help if he were taught."

"Take Lily to the victualling yard."

Averil ran out, leaving the door open. Miss Amy, seeing everything as usual from behind her shipbuilding yashmak of record-keeper, watched to see that the children were in the buoyant place of yard activity, warmed up the Shah with coffee, and said, "Mr. Jonson of Newcastle said of Mr. Armstrong that he swung like an erratic pendulum and if they call that poet's licence then no wonder you wouldn't find Wordsworth musing on ships when everything has to be true down to a millionth of an inch. In any event, Mr. Armstrong invented the hydraulic crane and he was away. He set up shop 'on the verdant western banks of Newcastle'—that's what they said, it makes you laugh now—'with a handful of mechanics.'" She got up and looked out of the window at the men about their business. At Averil, whose knot efforts were misunderstood by the shivering Shah as being due to English upper-class horse-whipping.

"Well, I ask you. Verdant banks. A verdant bank would be a distinct sign of laziness in this city now. We've no time for lazy dogs here, though I daresay they have their place in the South."

She opened a book of diagrams and showed him the drawings for capstans, dock gates, swing engines, cranes, window engines, and many another of the wonders of the time. "Watching the Crimean War, Sir Douglass's father saw how cumbersome the guns were. He pondered and after the Battle of Inkerman he sent to the government a design for a rifled breech-loading gun that weighed only three pounds. Things went up and up. By the time the British Association came to Newcastle in 1889, not so long ago, North-East shipbuilding led the world. Sometimes more than forty percent of the whole world total. Our machine engineering was second to none. British shipbuilding on its own was producing four out of five ships launched in the whole world and this coastline of forty miles, as I say, was producing forty percent of that whole world total! Well, you can imagine the pride. We were able to hold our own in economic doings as much as in the might and main of the military limb, as you can see from the Boer War, Your Royal Highness, and now from the threat of the Kaiser's war, in spite of the terrible spill of blood. You can put it down to our oil, our iron, our water. You can put it down to the number of people who want to get to Australia and America by our reliable ships, a steady thrum on the way being a good send-off to people with the itch for travel, not to speak of the black sheep, and I don't know a respected family apart from the Douglasses that doesn't have a black sheep. I'll say that again. You mark my words. The Douglasses are never going to have a black sheep."

Averil indeed marked and remembered the words a generation later.

"But for all the coal and wool and what-not," said Miss Amy, gazing at a diagram of how the old tea schooner's halyards worked, "you have to put it down to more than that. You have to put it down to the hardworking geniuses like Mr.

Armstrong and Sir Douglass. That's where our strength comes from and soon it'll be the women. It's all been done without the help of the government. London doesn't pay much heed to the North. There was a nice bit in Shakespeare that Averil read to me the other day—"

"You remember it, Miss Amy—"

" 'Come the four corners of the earth and we shall shake them.' 'Shake' or 'shock,' I don't recall it to mind exactly, but the meaning's clear. I've got a theory that Shakespeare was a great traveller himself, like a born man of the North East. He didn't vegetate in Stratford, did he? He was always up and down to London. And you can tell he must have got himself up North or else he wouldn't have written all that about Harry Hotspur, our own great Percy of all the Percys defending Alnwick against the cattle raids with their bailliwicks and moat gates and drawbridges. Well, the Scots came marauding for cattle and blood, and now you've got people from all over the world coming up cap in hand for coal and armaments and chemicals and iron and most of all for ships. We're building not just for the British Admiralty but for every navy that matters in the world. At the British Association meeting of 1889, Mr. John Rowe said . . . Just a minute . . . oh, yes, yes, here. 'No mere verbal description of these vessels will convey to the mind the science, art, and skill which they embody, they must be seen and fully inspected to be appreciated.' "

"Things are flourishing even more now than in your British Association visit."

"Yes, and always shall."

The Shah simply shivered. Averil and Lily swung their legs at the oft-told tale.

"All the drive and imagination and faults of the great Victorian enterprise," said the Shah from his invisible throne that held him aloft above Europe and business. Miss Amy took him to be more kind than he was, and said, "Well, you'll be interested to hear what someone said about the magnificent last meeting of our Royal Scientists. They settled into their accommodation at the Royal Turk's Head Hotel, a place also much favoured by touring actors, for bed and breakfast, and attendance, two pounds nine a week, dinner in private room five shillings; or at Mrs. Cooper's in Elsdon Road, Gosforth (bed and breakfast, use of sitting room, bath, and piano—one pound a week). They perhaps might have agreed with an anonymous observer who wondered whether it was not all being achieved at a terrible cost, 'for it is unfortunate that Newcastle presents its least pleasing features to the casual eye . . . old tumble-down houses, blackened walls, a dingy river. The water is of a muddy brown and the many factories on the banks are of an unrelieved ugliness.' Well, I can't say I agree, but this is my home. You have to have faith in science. 'The chimneys of Consett smoking out sparks and flame, the care of the riveters in making tight double tight, the physique of our men which is so different from the pale and wizened look of the men in the mines.' Miss Lily, that's enough stones. Put them away."

Averil said, interpreting for her sister as she generally did, "She needs two different things to put them into because she's sorted out the ones she's washed from the ones she hasn't. Some of them are her favourites, all washed, and they shouldn't get separated."

"Well, I daresay that can't be difficult in a shipyard, hinny." Miss Amy retired and brought back, with the help of two outfitters, one oil tank that had recently been carrying oil and one that was ready for cargo.

"This one's been thoroughly cleaned and whitewashed. What you've got will hardly cover the bottom. But my suggestion is that you bring your sorted cargoes in wheelbarrow by wheelbarrow, which is more than heavy enough for you as it is, and then we can wait until the oil tanks are a third full each of them, which will make a burden worth taking back in triumph to Braw Fell. I'll keep it a surprise for your father. I haven't thought out the mechanics for it yet, but the foremen will help: you can put your trust in that."

Averil and Lily went out with Miss Amy into the cold that they liked, Averil tying her coat with a rope belt by a bowline knot and two half-hitches and Lily refusing Miss Amy's hand, picking up stones being her task.

"The pavings are rocky," said Miss Amy.

"Why didn't the Shah come? Are all Highnesses lazy?" said Averil.

"I expect he's cold."

"I don't think he likes ships ordinarily, but you can see he's interested."

"I'm glad of that," said Miss Amy. "For I'm taking up your father's time with this talk. To his distinguished visitor."

The bell in the yard went for the end of the men's break and Averil picked up a stone for Lily. "This is a good stone to have."

"To have by one. Yes," said Miss Amy.

A great ship was to be launched that afternoon. The slipway was being greased. Much other work was on the way. Five big contracts were going full blast. The riveters and anglesmiths and plater's helpers and ship's joiners and fitters were collecting in throngs. "No man is an island," said Miss Amy caustically.

"Who said that?"

"I don't know. But *we* are."

"Tell the Shah about the *Mauretania* to warm him up."

They went back into the shed and made some strong coffee for the Shah's sake. Miss Amy sat at her desk and reached behind her for another old book of clippings that she knew by heart, but she preferred to get things right.

"Of course a great turning point was the signing with Laird Inverclyde of Cunard of the contract for the *Mauretania*. Her sister ship the *Lusitania* was built on the Clyde. The *Mauretania* slid into the Tyne at a quarter past four in the afternoon of September 20, 1906. We used to be famous for cargo tramp vessels, colliers, oil tankers, and warships. Now we were engaged in one of the most difficult problems in naval architecture and marine engineering. The time of the fast lines had come. You should have seen the pride of her. One hundred ninety foot long, eighty-eight foot wide, and sixty foot draft."

Miss Amy rustled through the pages of a whole beautiful book devoted to the *Mauretania*.

" 'She had accommodation for five hundred sixty first-class passengers, five hundred second-class, one thousand four hundred eighty third-class, and eight hundred crew, each one of them with fifty percent more space than in any other Atlantic liner. A complete telephone system, electric lifts to take the passengers through the nine decks. Six hundred and sixty-four staterooms. The grand entrances and staircases, says the shipbuilder—' "

". . . sounding like a posh hotel pamphlet," said Averil.

Miss Amy went on, " '—are treated in the fifteenth-century Italian manner. The woodwork is French, the panels being treated with some of the finest figured wood that one could wish to see. The grand staircase unequalled in size and beauty on any vessel afloat and indeed it is worthy of any mansion ashore. . . . The rooms are panelled in straw-coloured oak in the style of Francis I. . . . The rooms are upholstered in deep pink and a fine sixteenth-century tapestry at one end gives an admirable effect. . . . The first-class lounge or music room is a noble apartment treated in that charming style which obtained in France in the last quarter of the century and of which the Petit Trianon is perhaps the most typical example. The arrangement of the panels, and the delicacy and design of the carvings and columns, might have been the work of Gabriel Rossetti or Morris, but the architect has, in his scheme of colour, been inspired more by the sumptuous furniture of the period than by the wall decoration, and that with the happiest result. . . . Sixteen pilasters of fleur-de-pêche marble with ormolu capitals and bases, a chimneypiece of the same materials, soft creamy curtains with coloured borders and three fine panels of French tapestry, produce a colour effect which leaves nothing to be desired. . . . The library or writing room . . . will probably be regarded by many passengers as being the most beautiful in colour in the ship. . . . The wall panelling is of sycamore stained a silver gray. . . . The smoking room . . . is greatly enhanced by the wagon-headed roof, which is divided into three sections and decorated with beautifully modelled plasterwork.' "

The Shah looked moved.

Miss Amy carried on: " 'There were two regal suites, each comprising drawing room, dining room, two bedrooms, bathroom, and private corridor; sixty-eight special state and en-suite rooms, an addition to the first-, second-, and third-class accommodation.' "

Miss Amy was talking now at speed. "A great day. We had at least eighty thousand people to see the launching. The launching weight was something never tried before—seventeen thousand tons. We used over two hundred and ninety hundred-weights of tallow, twelve hundredweights of train oil, and twenty-two hundredweights of soft soap to make her slip down the berth. Six dray chains on each side, one thousand tons of them, were used to pull her up. And on her maiden voyage she carried a consignment of two and one-half million pounds' worth of gold from the Bank of England to the U.S. Treasury."

Averil thought this might seem small cheese to the Shah, but he kept a good countenance. "New records were set on every crossing, and only the most minor delays for safety's sake in dock. And they say we can only build cargo vessels! It's her speed that always made her magnificent, apart from all the beauty of the furnishing."

Miss Amy paused in the run of her talk and then quietly said, "I wouldn't like it to be known around the yard, because they'd call me a loser, but my heart's often with the cargo ships working along at their own speed. Sometimes I wish Mrs. Pankhurst had got women to sea. . . ."

Averil said nothing, rubbing her rope calluses, which hurt, unusually, after a particularly rigorous session with the family oak tree, which Sir Douglass had moved to this new family place in Northumberland, huge roots and all, at a stage in its centuries-old life when it was said it could not be done. The engineering problems interested him and he studied forestry for two years before he did it. Old school friends sometimes said to him, "What are you doing?" and he would reply, "Oh, trees," or, "Oh, steam," having a taciturn frame of mind.

Miss Amy said, "Every now and again a great ship like the *Mauretania* will go into a period of invalidism, according to its adventure record. And then back into the plunge." Miss Amy paused to ponder and said, "To no other ship belonged that trick of hers—that thrust and dip and drive into the seas and through them which would wreck the rails of 'monkey island' with solid sea or playfully splattered salty water on the captain's boiled shirt as he took turns on the bridge before going down to dinner." Again the Shah looked chilled as Lily slipped out for another cargo of stones.

Averil pulled up Lily's socks and Lily immediately pushed them down again, preferring the rumpled look of a schoolboy to a governess-trained girl. Averil, of course, understood. They were sitting side by side on a beautiful old steamer trunk with their grandfather's name on it in faded gold lettering, swinging their legs against the leather straps.

"Steel got so short, Your Royal Highness, that we went into concrete. We'd experimented before and we hadn't liked it, but beggars can't be choosers. American firms went back into wooden shipbuilding because of the steel shortage. Well, Your Royal Highness, most of the big firms came out of the war with a heavy profit, but it started to dwindle. We've never recovered from the blow to tramp shipping. The peace has had a very disorganizing effect." To hide the fact that she was crying, Amy went to a corner and made a pot of the strong coffee that the Shah had brought among his presents from Persia. The little copper pot seethed with goodness and strength. All four of them had a draught of the coffee.

"You should have seen the tramps we built on the North-East, Your Royal Highness," said Miss Amy, sitting behind her typewriter for comfort's sake.

"I once went on one of our banana boats to the West Indies for my summer holidays, being fed up with Bank Holidays and ice creams and 'Daddy promised me a bow-wow' on the pier. It was a trial honeymoon, a trial of the conditions rather than any particular fiancé because I hadn't got one at the time, and I tell you that by the time we'd reached voyage's end I'd have said yes to any man in sight, what with the interest of the construction and the sturdiness of it all and the very clever nature of the ballast."

"And I daresay the romance of the bananas," said the Shah.

"Bananas never hold any romance for me, nor any other fruit, though I can certainly savour the smell of a crate of pineapple. I daresay you could put it down to the lure of diagrams. It's something I've always felt. The best birthday present was compasses, both kinds, and a pair of dividers. I would then have been six. Every map we had to hand was pinpricked with

81

these divider points. I thought I knew how to get to the Canary Islands with only one refuelling stop, at Lisbon. They still use that route. I didn't invent it, of course, but I thought I had."

There was a mumble of gibberish from Lily, with a sailor's salute, to which Averil replied in the gibberish perfectly understood between them; and then Averil, who felt the need sometimes for explanations between friends, said to the Shah, "Lily wants to ask you whether there is a sailor skirt in Persia." Tears welled up in Lily's eyes when the Shah shook his head: she had seen, in this far country, a chance for combining her duty to Captain Averil and her duty as a woman stone mason.

5

Sir Douglass had become surprisingly acceptant of Averil's and Tess's political doings. He was proud of Tess, proud of Averil. He found in them the origins of that mutinous spirit that alone could subdue the starvation and violation he saw in worlds beyond his own. Himself a natural Socialist, though bred to be a Tory, he burned about Mrs. Pankhurst in America. Before the war she had three fund-raising tours to America, blistering audiences into some augury of pop-music rapture by announcing with a yell and an even greater than visual smoulder of her eyes, "I am what you call a hooligan." That caught the attention of American journalists after war had broken out in Europe. Using jingoism with the usual patronizing sound of tabloid newspapermen, they saw her fury as the mask of the bulldog British fighter. Few people perceived pathos in her muddleheadedness. She spoke about the peril of the "abstractions" of Socialist intellectuals: "Men like Bernard Shaw, Sidney Webb, and Mr. Graham Wallas, some of them very irresponsible—of the long-haired pale-faced type, men who worked up all kinds of visionary ideas about human beings, but have had no practical experience of human life, of the workingman or the employer." She insisted that only the women of England had sustained the political amnesty between the sexes during the age of women working in munitions. Only they had stuck to the job in hand of winning the war. American women, she was sure, would do the same.

Tess early persuaded Douglass to let her take Averil to a meeting of Mrs. Pankhurst's at Queen's Hall down in London. America, Mrs. Pankhurst reported, was sound. "Her whole idea is a peace dictated in Berlin." Tess and her daughter held a long discussion on the slow train back to the North. "That didn't sound right to me about Berlin, Mamma. Mrs. Pankhurst's part."

"Well, darling, stargazers playing the role of prophets often go too far. Open the picnic basket. There may be merit in going too far."

"But not in the wrong direction."

"Even the King and Queen don't know the right direction. All they can do is plant potatoes, getting very hot and tired, and ban alcohol in royal households for the duration as an example of self-discipline." She paused. "And then of course there are the parties for convalescent soldiers at the Palace."

"To honour and investigate them before they get hauled back to the trenches," said Averil.

Tess gave her a long thin cigarette and a box of matches decorated by a peeress friend of hers. Averil read out the words on the matchbox: they went "Matches for your matchless boys at the front."

"What on earth?" Averil said after a wait, stalled.

"It's Lady Talbot's war. *Idea* of the war effort. She paints fifty boxes a day and sends them to the trenches to encourage the men."

"God help us."

"You shouldn't swear yet. You can when we've got the vote. It's all right to do it in front of me. About the matches, I know it's silly, but she's not in touch much."

Tess ate a butterless bun and said, spitting the bread into a lawn handkerchief, "Lady Talbot is now sending a dispatch of thousands of plum puddings and a thousand brown woollen sweaters to men of one of the Buffs with greetings from Lady Talbot on a card pinned to each sweater. She also sends soccer balls, being convinced herself that the manliness of soccer is at the root of the British character: the character, that is, of the other ranks. She would not have sent rugby footballs."

She paused, and went on: "The *Manchester Guardian* ran the story of some titled woman who went to work in munitions. After she'd been at it for a month she gave a dinner party, wouldn't you know. She had a cabinet minister's wife and a working woman, which was her great social *coup*. She introduced her as 'Mabel, my mate in the shop.' The peeress and Mable wore print frocks with turbans covering their hair to add the distinctive munitions flavour, and the table was covered with lino as in the canteen. I wonder what the butler made of it."

"Probably relieved about being let off the laundry."

"The guests helped themselves to the vegetables, though the meat was served by a maid. 'Mabel and I get fifteen bob a week and it won't run to more,' said the hostess. Oh, yes, you mentioned the butler. The *Manchester Guardian* said he'd been sent to the theatre to get him out of the way."

"Going to the theatre is putting yourself in the way, though, if it's any good."

During the war, the Despard Arms opened in Hampstead Road, where Mrs. Pankhurst had lived in her presuffragette days. It offered food and fortifying drinks to men and women as well as giving entertainments, offering club rooms, some living accommodation, and bathrooms for public use. The redoubtable Mrs. Despard, a creature from the land of waxed fruits and antimacassars, hoped that the place would be the first of many of its sort. She wanted it to be a public house without the reproach of the name. The South of England groaned, but only faintly. The North-East, in the midst of a depression of already forty percent unemployed, took such an aspiration more solemnly, as folly. It gave a bad name to women's rights, the feeling ran. The women of the North had battled for generations. The rallying cries of the South were stale whispers up here. From the North, most of the South looks stultified and tame. Women in the pubs were a commonplace, drinking beer with their men or with each other. They scrubbed the doorsteps of their cottages every morning until the stone was white as the blocks of salt that were put out in the sheep country for the sheep to lick. One woman said: "It sounds a bit daft, a pub without beer, and I wouldn't fancy public bathing. Haven't they heard of a tin tub and a pump down there? After I've got my dad's bath ready I leave him to himself and get him a fish for his tea as usual. Sometimes a bit of bacon. He puts it between two good slices of bread and calls it a bacon sammer before he cleans the table to make the flies for his fishing."

"There's quite a bit extra to be earned with flies," said her friend.

"It seems there's a lot of flies if you're a man. Alan has a collection that engrosses him. Not being a fly-killer, he waits till they're nearly dead come winter and catches them at the last hop, when their wingspan's still intact." There was the usual Northumbrian silence of nearly twenty minutes and then her friend said without any trace of the odd in her voice but suppressing humour with difficulty, "John's the same with trout until his hand's cold enough. He's got a thermometer on the watch I gave him from Fenwick's last Christmas. He doesn't want to burn the fish. Seems silly to me when he's going to kill it, but he says it makes the difference, that meeting a human hand underwater. Afterward the fish is gasping, he says, and doesn't know. Many a thing we don't know. If you ask me,

I can smell the usual happening up here: no work, getting the slag in, and the politicians all carrying on down South about civilization."

"A lady suffragette who knew Mrs. Pankhurst came all the way North and asked why my curtains were turned to the street."

Her friend said equably, "And doesn't she know? How else would you hang a curtain so that it speaks for itself?"

"Daft. She meant well."

"We could have a ruby port and lemon."

When Tess's elder sister Catherine had died and left the literary decisions in her will to her niece, Averil found a suffragette flag neatly rolled up in her aunt's drawer of linen handkerchiefs scented with the smell of lavender sachets. In a desk drawer she found a bundle of papers from a suffragette friend of her aunt's. On thin and uncharacterized paper drawn from pads that could have been meant only for the use of prisoners or scriveners, there were long letters from women going through forcible feeding. One in particular struck her. It was quite a screed, obviously transcribed at pains through a long evening at the cleared wooden table of a great house. The ruled lines of the paper were pockmarked with dots of india ink where the writer had leaned heavily between thoughts, not necessarily at commas or full stops, dipping her pen nib into the bottle of Waterman's ink from, it seemed, the kitchen dresser shelf, except that this was a letter from a prison, where there could only have been a bed as narrow as a ship's padded-cell bed, a table, and a rickety chair. The letter read:

> Dear Miss Catherine, all is well here and we are holding
> our own. The doctor came yesterday for the forcible feed-
> ing which is no joke in these circumstances and he had

the cheek to come in with his hat on and I knocked it off saying didn't he know how to behave in the presence of a lady.

And there we have it, thought Averil, not crying: a suffragette going through forcible feeding for equal rights but asking for the minor gallantries of gentlemen to ladies.

We saw him act the same way, all of us when we met for exercise, no one to treat with, which is a help in the case of these indignatories and you will catch my meaning. Now there is something I want to tell you and I don't know how to go about it except with the facts which knowing you will be understood. I wanted to go to church this morning not for a breather or anything like that but because Sunday is not a day to be a spoilsport whatever cause you are catching your breath for and I have to say that sometimes my heart feels it is going to burst out of my bodice for the gasping probably due to the doctor's interferences but life is always an effort especially a new life like the one we are trying to make and how I love my country in spite of all this I think quite a lot of the men are with us and here the battle is going on more than anywhere else to build a better state it will be our new Jerusalem among the dark satanic mills. Well as I was saying I wanted to go to church. They have taken my cameo of the Crucifixion off my neck for fear I would put the pin which is quite sharp into my throat as though anyone of us would do such a thing the whole point is that we are alive to cluster round each other and rejoice in the undoubted ending of our efforts no true effort is without a true reward but I have to tell someone this. As you know I have been five weeks on those throat pipes without any food passing my lips but they presented me with a dilemma. The doctor the one whose hat I knocked off for his rudeness said I could go to church if I had a cup of tea and a piece of bread and butter now I agreed and I had it though leaving the crusts and I don't know whether I did the right thing I yielded to authority I suppose but I don't know PLEASE DON'T TELL THEM AT HEADQUARTERS AT LINCOLN'S INN FIELDS AND PLEASE HELP ME WITH YOUR USUAL KIND THOUGHTS. Yours in sisterhood Annie Lilley. P.S. I would like to write this in violet ink but they only give us the usual bleak Waterman's it will be Valentine's Day by the time you get this so here is a flower and a heart with an arrow through it if I could lay my hands on a card this heart would have a thorn through it in our case. Did I do wrong yours sincerely Annie.

Like the rolled-up suffragette flag, a small one, tattered, on a splintering bone stick, this letter, like the many others with it, was scented with the lavender sachets of the neatly stacked handkerchief drawer. In the same drawer Averil found a letter on stiff blue paper with an engraved letter heading from Government House, Gibraltar.

Forgive this strange writing paper! Will explain. Mummy is worried about the baby lion at Lynch-Sutton and wonders if you could bring a godmotherly eye to bear on him while I am in the midst of our work. I am wondering about my younger brother's idea of a Children's Order of Chivalry. You know he died when he was nine. His idea was that each of us lucky ones should adopt a child of the poorer classes corresponding with it in age. What do you think? As to the baby lion, it is on the drawing-room sofa, or should be, given that there is no meddling. He scratches leather but leaves velvet intact, and the dear thing draws in his claws at the feel of it. I think he may be lonely without us while we are slaving away at our meted tasks. As to myself, I am *not* very proud of myself and despair of robustness while darling Mummy slaves away tirelessly at her task of improving the lot of agricultural labour. His idea is to draw "the three strands" of agricultural life together—landlord, farmer, labourer—in a mood of common understanding. It seems to me a noble understanding and not *at all* like the feudalism we rightly find specious now. God forbid that any touch of it should taint Mummy's enterprise. (In the view of others.) Again I am wandering from the questions I know you will be asking. Here in Bad Kissingen I hear little from Lincoln's Inn headquarters but I hope to hear from you about all our commanders directly. I find the Continent heavyhearted and lacklustre, which is why I write to you about the baby lion, knowing you will nurture him as if he were your own. What a thought! You with a baby lion when you haven't even got a son! Mine both seem so old now that I have almost forgotten their parentage. They are rather handsome and *bon vivant* escorts! As to myself, again, I have been out for ten minutes in a nice yellow bath chair and am none the worse for it.

Yours ever in affection and sisterhood,
Antonia

P.S. I go next with mother to St. Moritz and Cannes, health being so fugitive, and then to our beloved English seaside. I am much enslaved by the notion of improving and *enlarging* our soup kitchens, the invalid kitchens, in the slums of London, so intend to face the fog come what may. I can feel myself ready to fling myself into this and forget my dear sons. Mummy will become the best grandmother in London. I am thinking of sending a hospital unit of nurses and surgeons to Russia to advise the Russians of our capital goodwill in the dreadful circumstances of their troops. What think you? I have in mind the first floor of the Grand Duke Dimitri's palace on the Nevsky Prospekt. There will be trouble from our fellow-countrywomen of nebulous goodwill who have constructed a refugee hostel of what appears to be hacked-up orange crates, or perhaps of the wood so hauntingly sawed off in the sounds off-stage in *The Cherry Orchard* itself.

And there was also a letter from an American, a trained mid-wife nurse, most celebrated for her aplomb as a pioneering lady motorcyclist. She had brought, to the handkerchief drawer's pile of documents, news of an effort to apply force in America passively by refusing to pay income tax or fill in census forms.

We feel a long way away from your struggle, which of course is so intimately connected with the war. God help us if America is condemned to be isolationist. But we read your pamphlets hungrily, as though you were sending us in return your own food parcels to us. You must know so little of the struggles in our own dark satanic mills. You would be particularly moved by the songs of the hillbilly women in their union struggle. America bursts easily into song, not only among the slaves so lately freeborn. It is our natural power of speech. I send you some verses I have written out on the backs of mill pamphlets, but they mean little without the music and the sight of these hillbilly women facing outward, always outward. I once asked a great Russian dancer why she thought it was that there are such leaps in Russian ballet, and she replied that it was because there was so much ground to cover. I think the same is true in our vast continent of the reach of human voices, stretching out to both the oceans, stretching far beyond the possibility of the human-voice register. The women sing as they wait for an accident at the mills to be resolved, not knowing whose relatives are dead, facing away; singing to each other. I have never seen anything like it. They are quite still, and only the voices gasp. I suppose we can find the roots of the style in slave music. But one has no feeling that these women are slaves. Perhaps it is true of this continent filled of people fled from pogroms that it is the one place that has been truly chosen to be populated rather than to be born in. That is why our mill women sing outward across such clear air. A long way to go.

Yours,
Alice

6

As Averil grew up, it was people like this to whom she felt kin. She had enough pocket money (saved in her sailor-suit pocket, stitched by her so that there was the narrowest hole for possible accidents during somersaults and handstands with Lily, who furiously tucked her dresses into her matching knickers)—she had enough money put by to make a flight fund for the two of them to escape to Newcastle. Miss Amy knew where they were, and told Sir Douglass, who cleared his throat and let things be. They took a small room in Gosforth and paid their rent by working in the kitchen. Averil bought, for ten pounds, a share in a printing machine. The binding of her pamphlets had to be done by hand, which meant the hand of Lily. Lily hated sewing because of its link to petit point and other loathed embroideries, but she did this for the cause. It was not the cause of down South, from which trumpet-cries echoed about "demarcation obstacles," but the cause of here and now where the grass was growing apace in the shipyards. They printed, with properly unspoken scorn, the report of a Hamburg shipowner who gave his reasons for Germany's success in shipbuilding as:

1. Less pay
2. Longer hours of work

3. Widespread piecework
4. Labour-saving machinery and no restrictions
5. Demarcation lines: none
6. No redundant labour.

The sisters put a very heavy full stop after the sixth clause. No redundancy. Yes, a state devoutly liberated, but no one but a German yard-owner, they felt, could decree the first two clauses, let alone the fourth and fifth.

The girls sat up late at night in their digs. They knew that their father knew that they were all right, through the delicate contacts of Miss Amy; and they recognized his filibustering and tender nature well enough to know that he would be satisfied. As they had brought few clothes with them, Averil was dressed prominently in her sailor suit, which she washed twice a week, to the detriment of the flannel, and ironed it with a flatiron heated on the range. The smell of clean and quite possibly scorched laundry reminded them of home, for which they were heartsick, and irritated their landlady. Lily continued to wear her homemade flowered dresses but cut them off below the waist to tuck them into her riding breeches, which she tucked in turn into thick long golf socks, having seen and been enraptured by a photograph of George Bernard Shaw. The prettiness of his voice—she could only think of it as that—contrasted with the rasping mood of his sentiments. Herself gentle, she was quite overcome by the weavings of his irony and emulated him by achieving the nearest she could to knickerbockers and by riding a bicycle.

The immediate problem was the dining-room wallpaper. The sisters were allowed to eat Sunday lunch—Sunday dinner—with their landlord and landlady, to help cook the Yorkshire pudding under the drippings of the delicious small cut of beef.

One Sunday after Lily had carried in the roast, she carved it herself, drawn beyond the circumstances of manners by the carving steel that she, a stone mason, knew full well how to use. The carving was perfect but the wallpaper was not. This wallpaper was mid-blue and poppled, like wet blotting paper, and blotting paper was what this blue wallpaper behaved like. The grease drops from Lily's carving accomplishment flew onto the paper and spread into the shapes of squashed beetles and the splatters of ink that can be shot by an adept schoolchild equipped with a nib pen, ink, and a wedge of blotting paper. It was not the sort of catastrophe that could be covered up. Lily apologized, Averil apologized, and a grim Sunday dinner was eaten, with the landlord carving the second helpings with stingy skill.

It was, of course, necessary to pay up. Averil, child of optimism, offered to repair the dining room in another paper if they wanted. She bought samples of what she and Lily liked, and of what she thought the owners would like, from Newcastle shops. She even got Miss Amy to find a roll of the flocked wallpaper that Sir Douglass had painted over because of the poisonous fumes of wallpaper glue. But, no, nothing would do but the same hideous pimpled wallpaper. Lily put Averil on the crossbar of her bicycle—like her sister, she would not be fobbed off with such girls' genteelisms as hopping onto a bicycle past the saddle instead of swinging her leg over it—and they found the selfsame wallpaper. With hatred, they paid the right amount (allowing for accident) and went to work on a trestle table in the dining room. The mess was stupendous. Both girls were innovators, not cleaners-up, though by three in the morning when the dismal wallpaper was up they realized the need of what Hilda Lauderdale had always called "cleaning up after yourself." It was an edict that Hilda herself carried out to the word, and the girls, weak, followed her example. They were weak not only with physical effort but also with tired giggles about the way the poppling of the wallpaper at least masked the bubbles of amateur paperhanging. Upstairs, rigid with dislike of their lodgers, who seemed to be capable of enjoying themselves in the most defeating circumstances, the landlord and landlady lay in their twin beds, alert to any sign of fun as plainclothesmen are to signs of a security leak. An escapade was having its way: drab and porous wallpaper was offering unofficial licence to the enemy Lady Rich.

The sisters split in time: Lily to sculpture in a field where she made enormous outdoor pieces and slept in a cottage that she had converted herself from a shepherd's lambing shed; Averil to work for woman suffrage and to carry on writing and printing her pamphlets. Sir Douglass installed, not a telephone, but a long-range electrical gadget that operated between the girls' two bedrooms and that set off a bleeper around Miss Amy's neck. In its own way, this link between the sisters lasted until the first to die, Lily, lost her considerable strength from pneumonia. Averil was there. So was her best friend, Andrew Corfe, later to be knighted, a slight, formidably featured man with a nose like a pen with which one would sign peace treaties rather than write bread-and-butter letters. Andrew insisted on going with his wife, whom he loved, into the morgue of the hospital. He was afraid that Averil would be angered by the religious appendages—the candles, the laying-out itself in a chapel—but at that point he did not know Averil very well. A small lace handkerchief over Lily's face looked, oddly, appropriately ladylike.

So it goes. Averil lifted up the handkerchief after a time and kissed her sister on the cheek.

"She's not there," said Andrew.

Averil said nothing, not even in her mind. After a while she said, "She was reaching out her right hand. I don't think anyone was with her when she died. She needed someone. Even a nurse. At five-fifteen this morning there should have been a night nurse."

As they left, Andrew walked a little behind Averil. She thought it was because she was going too fast and said in anger, without looking back, "I'm sorry, I can't go slowly." Her habit, now, as Lily's.

At the top of the slope, she turned abruptly and went back to the chapel, though not into it: three times, backward and forward. She picked up a stone on her last journey, inspected it, threw it away, and put her hands deeply into the pockets of her suit, still and always modelled on naval uniform. This stone would not have been particularly to her sister's liking. Memorabilia, and such.

Andrew and Averil had met at the first mixed working club in Newcastle. It was a Saturday night, and one of the sketches involved a man as Gertrude in *Hamlet* and a thin woman as Polonius. The gag was that the prompt book had been commandeered by Gertrude, who ran all the famous soliloquies together in unremitting rancorous tones. "To be or not to be" made it quite clear that it was certainly not to be. The lady, plump-thighed and formidable, had snitched "To sleep, perchance to dream" for her own purposes, being very much for sleep. This affected her attitude to Polonius, whom she felt to be an insomniac and therefore a faulty member of the society of Elsinore. Neglecting the care of her son, she regarded Polonius as the most damning example of the results of a man having his nose in a book. Gertrude very much wanted to wear Wellington boots for Ophelia's drowning scene.

"I'd never have let the news just be brought to me. We

97

could have saved that poor girl. She needs an object in life. If I'd been there in my Wellies, I could have pulled her out of it all. Nobody was telling her that she was being selfish. Her parents didn't understand her and nor did Hamlet: a genius, of course, the only convincing one in literature, but not an open understander. Poor girl, caught up in Victorian flower mania."

Averil and Andrew, after initial efforts, found themselves silenced by the performance. Averil had given up and was sitting having cider near the prompt side.

"You're on the prompt side," said Andrew awkwardly, hovering to join her.

"Not that I'm in any fear that Gertrude will forget anyone's lines. Oh, dear, what's she carrying now?"

"A fishing net."

"For after the drowning scene, I suppose. Christ, it will commandeer everything."

"Will she fight Laertes with it?"

"And throw away the goblet?"

"I once saw a very clever Ophelia who I thought could play Hamlet—she had the rancour and the furious intelligence—but I never thought I'd see Gertrude commandeering Hamlet," said Andrew. "May I sit down?"

With little incident apart from his buying her a better bike, they moved in as a couple with the formality of a Woolworth's curtain ring as a wedding ring. Andrew too approved of girls swinging their legs over bike saddles instead of tripping through. More panache.

Averil went home with the news.

"Why?" said Sir Douglass to Averil. "My blessings on you, darling, but I thought you didn't believe in marriage."

"Common-law marriage. Progressing maybe. What convinced me was his name."

"Which is what?"

"Corfe."

"Very nice, but what about it?"

"His family's best-known ancestor, a woman who was in a slit castle when the Romans were here and her husband was away fighting somewhere or other and she defended herself by pouring boiling oil on the heads of the marauders."

"It sounds a radical way out, considering we weren't yet at the Crusaders."

"She was ahead of her time. Her sheep had been stolen, her cattle had been stolen, and all she had was this oil that she had to boil herself because the serving girls were all of a twitter because the drawbridge had been hacked away and they couldn't swim."

"Of course they couldn't, but Mrs. Corfe of course could," said Averil's father. "The ancient Mrs. Corfe, the Mrs. Corfe who burned the oil. Cooked the oil."

"That's it, you see, she could do things."

"Could the present Mrs. Corfe? Would you come in and look at the order books?"

Together they went through the order books and the cash books. Three hours they spent together. One of them, and neither will ever be sure of which one thought of it, for they were much alike, worked out the costing for a tramp boat of more nimbleness than any the yards had built before, and one to take the tender away from Japanese competition.

"Well done," said Sir Douglass at two in the morning, pulling together the cord of his Chinese dressing gown. "Now, Averil, would you take off your sailor suit? In case it's creased, there's a little invention . . ." Averil took off her sailor suit and wondered grimly if this was what being a married daughter was like. So she said it. "Incest."

He said benevolently in a bawl from down the hall, "Not at all, no, no, not at all, it's simply for the sake of the new iron."

99

* * *

After a time, with Averil by this time quite invigorated in her camisole, Sir Douglass came back with a complicated and heavy mechanism, the bottom half designed to grip cloth and puff steam at it from below and above it, a boat-shaped and very big iron attached magnetically to its steam partner.

"The boat shape is not in memory of the yards," said Sir Douglass. "It is to enable the iron to press pleats and tucks and difficult corners at each end of the sweep. To cut into the storm, as it were, both fore and aft. The bulk must be centred. Aforeship and in the bows, the need is for speed and manoeuvre."

He put the sailor suit on an ironing board that was beside the silver fire-dogs and set something like a kettle to boil that would feed into the iron.

"Pleats or folds?" he asked.

"Pleats, please."

Would marriage ever be like this?

After three or four hours of work, Averil far from dropping, ingenuity triumphed. Her ringlets hung loose because of the steam in the room, but the sailor suit was done.

"It took us a while because it's a new mechanism to me," said Sir Douglass, "but we've got a perfect garment. A skilled worker would have done it in ten minutes. You see the advantage of the point, fore and aft? Curious that no one else hit on it for all these centuries. It enables one to make grand sweeps in the midst of a stroke and yet to judge the manoeuvring power to within an eighth of an inch when it comes to pleats and tucks."

No man to make ignominious distinctions between habitually male and female groups of words, he bethought himself of the rhyming word "cleat" in sailing and discussed it with his daughter. The ironing had been very much a joint enterprise.

"I bought the original components at Hexham and from among the scrap in the yard," Sir Douglass said.

Averil was sitting in her camisole, neither he nor she particularly aware of the fact. The sailor suit, spanking new, was hanging above the log fire "to get the last of the steam out of it." It looked fresh, except that Sir Douglass had contrived to make navy blue run into white around the collar.

"Tess will deal with it, will know what to do," he said, forgetting that his wife was now an invalid upstairs but remembering that she always had a solution for everything.

Averil said, "The cleats, *pleats* are superb."

"We've launched a new ship with this iron! I'm eager to mass-produce it. Think of what it could take out of the drudgery of ironing choirboys' vestments with that bowsprit. What a wonder that no one has ever thought of it before. The reason would be that the handle is set to take the weight at the back in the old-style form of iron, whereas it should be evenly distributed, exactly on the principle of a ship's tossing to and fro, in a more primitive way that no one seems to have hit on. Now, I think the reason for that would be that a woman naturally uses the heel of her palm as a weight-giver, whereas she should be given an instrument that allows her to use it lightly and with equality of balance."

"Or him."

"Or him indeed."

"As in *your* case, Papa," said Averil. "When you went to prison with Mamma, did they treat you well?"

"I had the poor advantage of being a man, so they wouldn't allow me to be forcibly fed."

"Were you mocked?"

"For being with your mother?"

"There weren't many husbands there."

101

"Idle jokes from London peers and the backwoodsmen in both Houses of Parliament. That was all. And a few more ugly bouts when we were on our way to jail. The officers were unpleasant. I tipped off the hat of an official who didn't take it off when he came into your mother's cell. She did the same. She said it was no way for a gentleman to behave, and she was quite right, for she was never anything but a lady."

"How many men were there? Forty at a time? Fifty?"

"Not that many. We were allowed in as a privilege. I believe there was a gentleman's agreement in the law that if a woman should pass out or die in the course of imprisonment, so long as her husband was with her it was accounted to be his fault. Of course, that made for a lot of soul-searching between couples, initiated by rather an unkind motive—condescending, we thought it—but it also made for a lot of trust if the couples seized the law in their own hands. Some husbands and wives never forgave each other. For the ignominy. Others never forgot it. I think you had better climb into your sailor suit because your mother is moving about upstairs. It's all sparkling fresh and new, thanks to our invention."

Averil's father, a little bent now at the shoulders but moving at speed, was out of the door in a second to the sound of his wife's movements.

"Tess?"

"Come up, darling. What have you been doing?"

"Averil's here."

"As if I hadn't heard. Don't bring her up, dear, I've got so bony. What were you doing?"

"Experimenting with my steam iron. The twin-bowed magnetic one I talked to you about last week when you were trying to sleep. It seemed to be a help to get you to doze off, for some reason."

Averil thought it time to take matters into her own hands

and went up to her mother's and father's room. Yellow, with white net curtains blowing in the dusk wind and her mother's portable writing desk opened up on her bed.

"Darling," she said to Averil, "and your father's ironed your dress. I thought he would. Prinked and pristine. What are you going to do about the navy-blue stain on the white of the collar?"

"Either we shall invent a perdurable dye," said Sir Douglass with a chairman's due dignity, "or Averil and I with the help of Mrs. Lauderdale will investigate the possibilities of a cube of Reckitt's Blue lightly sprinkled on the navy-blue stains to bring them back to white. One could use a nail brush, very lightly, with only a sprinkling of water on the brush. I believe it would serve. Hilda uses Reckitt's Blue to make the icing on her birthday cakes pure white. Just a smidgen. It isn't poisonous."

"Are you sure?" Tess said faintly.

"Can't you finish your nice supper, Your Ladyship?" said a housemaid, coming in for the bed tray.

"Tell Hilda the trout was very nice but that I suddenly thought it might have Reckitt's Blue in it when I realized it was blue trout."

"The whole house is obsessed with Reckitt's Blue!" roared Sir Douglass, stomping about the room in a tempest. "This great house might as well be an advertisement for Colman's Mustard! Don't you realize Her Ladyship needs rest and something more tempting to her forcibly fed throat than Reckitt's Blue or Colman's Mustard? Or to give honour where honour is due, anybody else's Blue or anybody else's Mustard, though I've yet to hear of them? Her Ladyship has been forcibly fed and her throat will never be the same, for she struggled like a tiger."

He glanced out of a window and wept.

"We've got to feed her up. And"—with the inconsequence that had carried him through many a board meeting—"any

103

Colman's children who come to the door asking to practice the piano are not to be allowed in."

"One of them is all right," said Tess.

"He's the one who doesn't play."

"He unplugs the pianola from the Bechstein."

"And plays the pianola. Dreadful sound he gets, no match for the invention of such a delicate instrument."

"No, it's the Bechstein he plays, darling."

"It makes no difference," said Sir Douglass, with the dismissal of hamstrung logic that his family knew.

"Papa tells me you're to be married."

"I am already. To a man called Andrew Corfe."

"His ancient forebear poured boiling oil onto the heads of Roman marauders. Not on the heads of the anti-Crusaders, you understand. A thousand years ahead of her time."

"What does he do, darling?" said Tess.

"He helps me with the mailing lists of the pamphlet. He works in his father's shipyard."

"Which yard?"

"Chalcott's."

"Ah," said Sir Douglass, counting debentures and contracts in his head, and coming to a quick conclusion about how to act in this period of world shift.

"Sound firm in rackety times. We're always happy to do business with them."

"I asked Miss Amy," said Averil, "and she thought very highly of them."

Sir Douglass lowered his wife's blinds and contemplated a hydraulic system to be installed all over the house that would automatically lower the blinds by an hour after sundown to save the maids work. After that pause, he tried speech again.

"You've been talking to Miss Amy behind my back?"

"Dearest," said Tess, "when you're working, all that anyone ever sees is your back."

"So when are you going to get married?" said Sir Douglass to Averil.

"We *have*. We *did*. Two weeks ago." Pause. "You could think of my newly pressed sailor suit as a going-away present."

Onset of the mock roar again; Tess and her daughter looked at each other; and Averil counted.

"Could the new invention be called the Corfe Cleaning Aid? Of course it doesn't actually clean, but it's a great aid to the crimping process"—walking around as she said the words, with her skirt whirling out into a ball in spite of its otherwise hidden design as a pair of trousers stitched together by Averil down the middle.

"As you see," she said, not at all breathless. Her mother leaned forward, full of eagerness after release from the blue trout, and said, "Yes, indeed."

"Andrew would do a lot else apart from the pamphlets?"

"His father's in shipping and so's he. I doubt he'll go South, however bad things get."

"They will," said Sir Douglass with true grimness.

Andrew and Averil, most happily married, bought and redecorated the ugly house in Gosforth that Averil and Lily had so suffered from: the one with the wallpaper.

"Was it mutton or beef?" said Andrew.

"Beef."

He peered at the new layer of blue pimpled wallpaper.

"Odd. It looks more like mutton to me. You see, it's coming through even this layer, the meat-fat stains. Why didn't you take off the old layer before you redecorated?"

"Oh, Andrew, there's just so much time to be given to wallpaper."

105

"Look at this. I'd swear it was mutton."

"Well, we were here, and it was beef."

"I've never seen beef fat behave in this way, and I spent my whole childhood with sheep. That is, live mutton."

"What do you think we did?"

"Look at this mark. They all look like continents. That man Rorschach is on the wrong track. None of these marks make me think of spiders or elves or Mamma's womb. They make me think of South America or India or South Africa. The great landmasses. Does that mean I should have emigrated?"

"This one looks like Tasmania, and nothing, not even you, will ever persuade me we should have or ever shall emigrate to Tasmania. It's curious that none of the blotches, these vague and really very well-covered blotches, should look like England as seen in beef fat—"

"Mutton fat."

"Covered by pasta but still seeping through. You'd think that England would seep through anything in our case."

And duly they had a son, Tony, a lovable boy with hair that his father proudly described as making him look like some wretchedly self-commending advertisement for yeast extract.

"No, darling," said Averil, "he's born to be the model for that nighttime drink for children that the advertisement sells with a very dodgy question. 'Is your child a highly strung child?' Do you know of any parent, a single parent in the whole world, who isn't convinced that his child is highly strung?"

But Tony was not highly strung. He was the cotton-wool in God's ears coming down from a height, deafening to prayer.

7

Averil and Andrew, indubitably in love, took Tony out to a Chinese restaurant in the docks of Newcastle. Where ships come, Chinese cooking is, even at the beginning of a terrible recession when weeds looking like herbs grow up through the cracks in paving.

Andrew was working eighteen hours a day at his father-in-law's business, where he had been given a minor place in the hierarchy, thinking it more safe and more kind not to be working at a higher level at his rival firm of Chalcott's. Averil and he ordered wonton soup and fantail shrimp and fried rice for the three of them. Tony, slung in a papoose alternately round his parents' necks, was now aged four and a half. He was put in the papoose for what his parents regarded as his shelter. He wanted plain shrimp and plain rice, and he got it. He then trotted around the restaurant offering what was all too plainly part of his baby leftovers to any others who were there.

Any others. An official-looking sign read: IT IS ILLEGAL, IN THE INTERESTS OF FLOOR-BURDEN, FOR MORE THAN 140 PERSONS TO BE PRESENT IN CASE OF FOX-TROTTING OR OTHER. As there were, at most, eight people in the restaurant at any one time, apart from a policeman who came in ostensibly to watch over the safety of the neighborhood but actually to pick up some carry-away egg rolls, neither illegality nor danger weighed. A strange order of mounting risk.

The place was run by Mr. Chee and Madame Chee. It was a naturally acclimatized sample of the stamina that carried the North-East through the Depression. Little or no business; perfect, exhausted mannerliness; no drop in standards of eggs rolls, no shift in equilibrium of the ethics of service. Mr. Chee, a tiny, active man with a mouth that seemed to have been drawn upside down, but implying no loss of kindliness, ran the bar. Few frequented it. To hang around a foreign bar was too close to the bone in these days of poverty. On this particular evening, when Averil had been working at the printing shop with Tony in the papoose on her back to keep his fingers out of the printing-shop machines, Mr. Chee was serving three seamen and helping Madame Chee with a crisis in the kitchen. The cook, temperamental as cooks will be, had suddenly objected to the heating water of the eighty-year-old waiter being on the cook's very own burners in order to heat the waiter's few orders for hot rice wine, and had admonished him to the extent that the waiter was forced to use hot tap water to surround the pretty little pottery rice wine holders in a series of cardboard beakers meant to hold tea for customers in the cinema next door and kindly lent in sympathy with such rows as spring up in times of sore economic need. The octogenarian waiter, muffin-faced, giggling with the beneficence of the ancient all-knowing that, in the Chinese, often reminds of a baby born of hope, shuffled laughing with an unstable tray of rice wine to Averil and Andrew, bowed, and upset a little of the lukewarm tap water with his shaking hand. Tony watched gravely. Being only four and a half, he did not yet make it clear whether his observation of the mistakes of others was critical or in alliance. He held this right of masquerade close to his chest for several years.

* * *

And in the meantime, Madame Chee worked at her desk with the carry-away orders. She stood at least an inch higher than her husband, but their sizes were still in tune with the heights of their adopted home, with the members of the hungry North-East generation where five-foot-one was average for a man who had been down the mines for years and was now on the dole. Above Madame Chee's cashier desk hung a colored hand drawing of a woman remarkably like her, actually the young Madame Chiang Kai-shek but done with obvious clumsy love of Madame Chee by a hand-drawing expert from Newcastle. There was a picture light above the portrait as though above a Botticelli. The plucked eyebrows of the sitter were raised to an unnatural quizzical angle; below, in a sharply molded gold lamé dress, the mountainous dainty incline of her breast strangely raised the lamé to two sharply questioning angles that matched the plucking of the eyebrows.

Tony struggled with and out of his papoose as soon as the food came. He seized the choices he had already made between plain and fried rice, between fried fantail shrimp and boiled shrimp, and leaped off his mother's knee with a plate of shrimp to play host to the very few other customers. To each of them, to his satisfaction and their discomfiture, he gave one shrimp and pointed out their bottle of soy sauce. He would not have agreed with Lamb, who in his own self-satisfied way wrote that the greatest pleasure he knew was to do a good action by stealth and have it found out by accident. Tony liked the accident to be seen, by him above all. It was a trait in him that troubled his tutor, though everyone else assumed that it would pass. But his generosity was indivisible from his masterfulness. He adored making beloved men of the unloved and to know that the craft was his. His character, still in the making and sometimes of sharp worry to his parents and adult friends, seemed to strangers to be founded in infant goodness, an instinct for the beneficent that was almost premoral. Few but his parents, tardy to find fault but in this case all too swift to mourn, saw in his baby acts of courteous divinity the roots of a man who could be engaged in excellence but be not totally the more attractive for it. Even at four and a half, he found one of the hands to whom he extended charity growing chill and drawing away. The delight in performing good offices was preternatural and not, indeed, so much premoral as antemoral. The baby's delight at the watchful giving of a shrimp could not, given the ethical sagacity of his face, a face whose expression seemed already at times to outweigh the infancy of his body, have been unaccompanied by knowledge of the fact that such pleasure imposes dutiful obligations on the shrimp-receiver. Hungry and kindhearted men, one or two of them, shoved the childish hand away; one or two others took Tony onto their knees and tried to unloose him back into babyhood by giving him crisp noodles. It was no good. He wanted seniors who would stare up at the authoritative sun of his gaze. He was ready to fight his own battles. He asked no help. He demanded a different sort of shrimp in order to have a sort of Maundy Thursday money to hand out, and when he wriggled off the receiving lap it was the hungry adult who was made to feel that he had failed, who had found the baby's benefactions tactless. Who would suspect a toddler of lack of tact?

In time Averil called upon the help of her old friend the Rector of Hexham. Andrew was gray with fatigue from the anxiety of working at the unemployed shipyards. Averil herself was trying to rally the wives of the men of the dole to use their vote, use their voice, but she found it difficult to rouse energy in women so weary with the mere morning beat of scrubbing their stone doorsteps chalk white and their collecting of free slag to make a hot range for their men when they were back from collecting round the pubs while their children, loose from the lead, were running like a pack of delighted insects in unfailingly crisply washed clothes over the slag heap. Dressed in bright dotted cottons, their minute figures made them look like lucky ladybirds. Catch one on your clothes, count the dots, and there will be that many years of ease ahead: in these times, not an accounting of the ladybird's dots, but one of any possible futures that lay ahead for the alighted-upon.

So the Rector of Hexham came, took tea with the pupil of whom he was much fond, absorbed the significance of the mean circumstances of her Gosforth house, and watched the child. Tony struggled off his mother's knee, dealt unkindly with the rarely afforded butter on a crumpet that he had decided to refabricate as a present, and gave it to the Rector. It was all too clear that the baby's strongest paternal affections would be habitually given to a man who admitted the moral height of the heinous toddler. The Rector shook his head, gave the rebuttered crumpet to Averil, and played the piano. Averil had two upright pianos given to her by her father, linked by a duet system of his own radiant devising that she had unlinked because Andrew didn't play. She relinked it, more out of love for her father than for music's sake, and the Rector and she played a double concerto for harpsichord. Tony sat on their feet alternately, and then uncharacteristically noticed that he was impeding their playing and wriggled to a short distance to listen. Perhaps all would be well.

Sir Douglass gave backbone to this thought. It seemed, in his optimistic presence, of all things sunny in this strongest of countries where shadows from clouds passing the sun cast patches of dark on the heather, that nothing could be other than for the best if it were done with force enough of far-

111

sighted hope. In his grandson he saw the future that, in mounting age, he wanted to endow.

He made what his benefactors later found to be a peculiar will. It laid down that Braw Fell and his fortune were to pass in trust through Averil for Tony and then only on condition that Tony had a child. Otherwise the house and the money were to go to the Society of Obstetricians and Gynecologists. However, no one in the family knew yet of the clause because he was not a man to use a will as a weapon. His seriousness about his inventions was now bent in greatest sobriety to the plight of his bailliwick, the shipyards. After long days when he often slept overnight in his office, he read one day something in Conrad, who joined the *Torrens* as second mate in 1891, twenty-six years after she was launched: the fastest ship on the Far East run, capable of reaching Adelaide in sixty-four days, the last full-rigged passenger clipper ever built. As a child he had found his words copied out in the first of his schoolbooks by his father, attributed to Conrad, with careful details and dates. Conrad had written that the way his ship had of letting "big seas slip under her did one's heart good to watch. It resembled so much an exhibition of intelligent grace and unerring skill that it could fascinate even the most unseamenlike of our passengers." The *Torrens*'s last passenger journey was taken in 1903 and she was broken up in Genoa in 1910. For Sir Douglass, to read of the breaking of a ship was like the breaking up of the mightiest endeavour of a private life. He was that more uncommon Englishman, a man whose boundaries were deeply English, but not England's.

Years later, in 1934, the great *Mauretania* was to be broken up. Sir Douglass was already a very old man but still running the shipyard as Chairman with his son-in-law, Andrew, as a director. The *Mauretania* had been built on Tyneside twenty years ago, in his own and its heyday. He remembered the less-sung glory of the *Turbinia* when she was built in Newcastle by an Irish aristocrat called the Hon. Charles Algernon Parsons. A nippy little ship, only one hundred feet long and capable of thirty knots, which stole the thunder at the Royal Review that marked Queen Victoria's Diamond Jubilee at Spithead. The ship suddenly capsized the splendour of the occasion by darting in between the splendid arrays of row A and row B of the fleet, which was ranged in four lines each five miles long. The Hon. Charles Algernon's little terrier upset the display of English war power. Chauvinism had known no bounds. *The Times* said that the review tomorrow "cannot fail to be one of the most characteristic and striking national ceremonies in celebration of the Diamond Jubilee. It possesses a significance which is directly and intimately connected with the welfare and prosperity of the Empire. . . . The fleet is certainly the most formidable in all its elements and qualities that has ever been brought together and such as no combination of other countries can rival." *The Times*, on the day, was not downcast, revelling in the fact that half of Europe, it seemed, had come to see the Prince of Wales inspect the fleet on behalf of his mother, of whom *The Times* had not in its bulldog power been at all fond on account of her retreat to Osborne during her widowhood. But as soon as the inspection was over, pomp was shaken by the terrier *Turbinia* slipping in and out of the rows of dowager warships. *The Times* was fearfully cross. "During the passage of the royal presentation the lines were kept creditably clear by the vigilant and ubiquitous patrol boats, but in spite of all their efforts, the now famous *Turbinia* defied authority. At the cost of deliberate disregard of authority, she contrived to give herself an effective advertisement by steaming at astonishing speed between the lines A and B shortly after the royal procession had passed." *The Times* spoke of her lawlessness. She was an early suffragette.

Next day, George Baden-Powell, addressing himself from the Carlton Club, wrote to *The Times:*

Sir,

Your correspondent at the great Naval Review writes of the remarkable performance of the *Turbinia*—"the fastest vessel in the world"—that she "contrived at the cost of a deliberate disregard of authority" to make a "brilliant but unauthorized" exhibition of "astonishing speed."

I happened to be on board the *Turbinia* at the time, and in justice to her designer, the Hon. Charles Parsons, and to Mr. Leyland, who were running her, I ask leave to state that the astounding runs she made between A and B lines on Saturday were in obedience to a message brought by a picket boat that the admiral wished her to show her best speed, more especially for the benefit of His Royal Highness Prince Henry, who was watching her from the German man-of-war.

The exhibition of speed, so far from being unauthorized, was specially invited by the authorities.

Experts will like to know that on this run the *Turbinia* topped the unprecedented speed of thirty-four knots. The most noticeable feature was the entire absence of vibration.

I am,
Your obedient servant,
George Baden-Powell

It was a very male row about mechanics that Sir Douglass, an era later, saw as appealingly and haplessly feminine. He was not going to have His German Royal Highness Prince Henry condescending to his Tyneside's *Turbinia,* any more than he was later to take FDR's patronage to the *Mauretania,* an attitude that smelled to him of the rank herring of male prejudice. Sir Douglass was a man who loved women: hence the character of Averil. The *Turbinia* was a woman ancestor of the *Mauretania.* FDR, disliking her with the leader's mixture of common zeal, arrogance, and a Victorian sermonizer's gift of tongue, again called her "The Queen with the fighting heart." Neither the size nor the speed of the vessel, he occultly again said, could have given the *Mauretania* her fame. That rested on something more intangible: on her personality. But he said, typically again, that he hated travelling in her. "Why? Heaven knows! Yet not for one minute did I . . . fail to realize that if ever there was a ship which possessed the thing called 'soul,' the *Mauretania* did." Sir Douglass found such anthropomorphism fatuous. People beset on work and gadgets generally do.

People beset on work. Averil's husband, knighted for the characteristic, was another. His mother, cross not to be a ladyship rather than proud of her son, was a Christian Scientist with a frigate-shaped bosom and a battleship mind. She played bridge with her son, deliberately choosing a game that her daughter-in-law did not know: croquet; clock golf; the piano (duets with her doctor), and the leading ladies in amateur dramatics (with her son as the ingenue, until Averil put her foot down). On Andrew's and Averil's honeymoon, his mother insisted on going with them to stay in the next-door room at their favourite hotel, the Railway Hotel in Newcastle, and loudly fainted outside their door at midnight. During their marriage she took to a couch, lying in vacant but not pensive mood against pillows scented with rosewater. Once, her son arrived, much tired with the acceleration of unemployment and at his wits' end as to what to do for the men in the yard, and she asked him faintly to look out of the window at her garden.

"How I love my garden."

"So you've said."

"I am inordinately *orgeuilleuse* about my delphiniums. How are my beauties?"

"No one, no one but you, could possibly have said that. You're looking a bit peaky."

"I'm ill with something. But there's no sensation in matter. It's all in mortal mind."

"Then what the devil are you doing on that couch?"

"Don't use that word, darling."

"What are you doing, though?"

"I'm holding the truth. Mortal mind has given me the false belief that there is poverty in Gosforth. A practitioner is holding the truth with me."

"Poverty! Blimey! Millions of men all over the country are out of work. Holding the truth, indeed. C.S. practitioners holding the tops of their noses and gulping cucumber sandwiches at a mile a minute and five guineas a go."

"Poverty is mortal mind. It's wrong thinking."

"Try saying that in the yards."

"Then mortal mind must reign in the yards."

"Christianity used to be about the virtue of poverty just as much as of chastity. Where did Mary Baker Eddy get this idea of the virtue of prosperity and of being chairman of the board? Because 'she knew the truth, and the truth shall make ye free.' "

"I wish you wouldn't be sarcastic, dear. It isn't funny."

"Mamma, Christian Science is the most idiotic religion that man embracing woman ever dreamed up. The term 'man embracing woman.' I doubt if Mary Baker Eddy ever countenanced the idea of an embrace."

"There it goes again, this sarcasm."

"Averil and I think Christian Science is funny as well as unkind."

116

"That confirms me." His mother shifted her pillows and smelled the rosewater. "Unkind, dear?"

"Being a good C.S., you simply haven't noticed the Depression."

"A depression is a belief of mortal mind."

"Ah, that."

"Those men are holding the wrong thought. It's animal magnetism. Dear, you do look gray. I don't think Averil is feeding you enough."

Two weeks later Andrew died of a virus brought into the docks by one of the seamen, or so the doctors said. His mother had refused at first to let Averil call in any doctor. "He's turning his face to the wall, dear. It's this Depression," she said with her customary mixture of faintness and opaque obstinacy. With his death, it seemed she felt no pang. "He's passed on, dear," she said to Averil, who had come round to see how she was. She was drinking a brandy and ginger ale, forbidden by Mary Baker Eddy but recommended by her practitioner because of combating the power of mortal mind. "Here's to my loved one on his journey," she said, lifting the glass, offering nothing to Averil.

Averil took Tony to Sir Douglass's. It seemed the best idea. Tony was always hell-bent on the hydraulic phaeton, being keen on the possible death of the driver and also on the process of murder of the red rhododendrons. This betook his lingering lethal mind to, not the death of his father and its effect on his mother, but a story he found entertaining.

"Grandpa," he said, looking seraphic in his minute gray flannel suit, "you know about the legless English pilot who was captured by the enemy and put in a German prison camp?"

"He's a brave man."

117

"The funny thing is that the Germans took away his legs, his iron legs, in case he ran away."

"You find that funny?" Sir Douglass did not, and confirmed Averil in thinking his guardianship salutary. He was not a burly Northumbrian, as his countrymen are generally taken to be. He had the stature of a divining stick and a twig-shaped chin that matched. If he had any bulk, it seemed to be the bulk of a stick wrapped in bandage as a tourniquet. He had acquaintance with grief. The plight of the yards weighed. Two weeks later his wife died, again apparently of some seaman's virus that would have been brought into the house by his being there. Averil stayed for a month, neglecting her work in Newcastle, giving different sorts of concentration to other things and to her father and her son by driving the phaeton around the paddocks.

"Mind the pullets," said Sir Douglass, as errant birds pretending they were horses galloped over the grass. Sir Douglass liked disarray in menageries.

"What's a pullet?" said Tony.

"A teenaged hen," said Averil.

"I bet it's not," said Tony.

Sir Douglass bent down under his legs and drew out *The Shorter Oxford English Dictionary,* the second tome. He looked up "pullet." "She's right," he said to his grandson.

"You like it when she's right and I'm wrong. Nobody cares if I'm right. Nobody cares about me at all."

Averil turned the last sentence into a melody that could become a round. Anything to lighten this leitmotif of Tony's. Anything not to have the sulks in an hydraulic phaeton. Anything for the sulks not to become confused with grief. Something had to be done about Tony. Sir Douglass did it by asking him that evening in his study what the boy most wanted to do.

"I want to go South. I wouldn't mind Harrow."

"There was an old lady. The Etonian boy offered to get her a

118

chair, the Wykehamist boy got it, and the Harrovian boy sat on it."

"Did you go to Winchester?"

"I was working in the yards by the time I was fifteen."

"I bet we couldn't afford it."

"Your mother works very hard. She always copes."

"And you could do an invention for me as a bequest in advance of your popping off."

"Or you could do some work for a scholarship," said his grandfather grimly. "Your mother would miss you less if you'd won your way. If you were doing what you wanted."

"That would be appeasing her guilt complex."

"She hasn't got one, whatever jargon that may be."

"It's Sigmund Freud."

"Who's he?"

"A Viennese psychoanalyst."

"You read psychoanalysis in the way a boy of your age should be reading books about sex." Sir Douglass paused. "Or childbirth. Your grandmother and I put a pile of books about childbirth in the attic thinking you'd want privacy. Now *there's* a bequest. I won't tell you where. You'll have to look. We thought you'd found them once when you were eight and we were playing hide-and-seek, and then your grandmother got worried by your silence because being in hiding can be frightening, and then you turned out to be eating three tins of sardines and refusing to share them with the other children in the linen cupboard. Your grandmother didn't like food among the linen. What was that about a guilt complex?"

"Mamma's got one about me."

Sir Douglass considered, playing with a page-turning invention. "No, she hasn't. She's got an innocence complex. And I don't like Northumbrians going South and losing their roots, but the sorry thing is that you never had any."

"Any what?"

"Roots. Apart from pulling up the red rhododendrons. Instead of replanting the soil around them. Your grandmother and your mother always paid attention. I wonder if we couldn't replant the soil around you." Sir Douglass waited for any response, but none came. "No, it's too late. It was always too late."

"I think I would rather like to go to Harrow."

"As I said, your mother will make things work. I can't see you getting a scholarship."

"She'll miss me, of course. But she'll be sending me a tuck box for contact."

"What *have* you been reading while she's been working?"

"She's not working now." Because of the infection in the house, every piece of paper that went out of it was fumigated in the oven and came out frail and browned. Averil felt as if she were in a house with the plague. She sent off Tony's application papers to Harrow as though from a house afflicted with the pox. She feared for the health of her father, who spent much of the day dialling Miss Amy at the deserted docks so as not further to infect her with the seaman's possible germ, pottering about with his new inventions and pondering.

8

While Tony was at Harrow, costing his mother a small fortune in monthly tuck boxes of sardines and sweetened condensed milk and jam and toffees and boiled sweets that he exchanged in bribery for prizes in squash racquets, she was working away again in some poverty and with some amusement at the Newcastle branch of the Despard Arms, which still provided poor people with food, restorative drinks, lectures, "bathrooms for public use," and other things designed by the high-bred planners in London to remove the popular meaning of "public house." Averil, for her part, clung to it, liking the ruby port and lemon mixtures, the goodwill, the Saturday cheeriness after a week of struggle, the easy admission at last of women to men's traditional domain. In tears often at night, that most difficult time of the twenty-four hours for the ill and the sad to live through, she read Swift and agreed with him about grief and public weeping. Yes, when he said that "there is something of Farce in all those Mournings, let them be ever so serious. People will pretend to grieve more than they really do, and that takes off from their own true Grief." People would sometimes ask her who her best friends were; Tony, when young, constantly asked her who her four best friends were; she would name five, in all truth: her hus-

121

band, her father, Emma in Jane Austen, Ivan Ilyich in Tolstoy, and Swift.

While Tony was tucking into his tuck box and asking for more, Averil was still living in the blotting-paper house in Gosforth and writing pamphlets. In spite of the flapper vote, and the reign of the gay young things of blessed fortune in London, things up North were not yet fine for young women. Magistrates liked to call them "thoughtless young girls"—a euphemism for prostitutes—if they were under nineteen and to send them to prison for suspicion of infecting soldiers (still "our gallant men at the front" in the manly mind, even in the thirties). Averil, a gay spirit, took it on herself to do something for the suppressed exuberance of girls, a word that she was to uphold in its original meaning all her life, just as she was to uphold "gay" in its age-old sense. We cannot, she thought, we simply cannot afford to lose any word that supports the blithe.

For the best part of two nights, she set herself the task of re-writing in words that would be debonair a severe apostrophe from an emergency Freedom League: "If a girl is regarded as guilty of crime, the blame falls on the society in which she lives. Gaiety, joy, harmless fun, have been taken out of her life, she spends her days working long hours in factories: is she to spend her evenings in mean and crowded homes, because the streets are desperately dangerous? The remedy is to make the streets safe. Build churches and gymnasia for the youngsters, teach them singing, dancing, acting, and art if you like, but do not crush the exuberance of life out of them." If you like, indeed. Yes, indeed. And right about the crushing of exuberance, but there must be a better way to put it. Averil worked hard at the task. Her nature was sunny, and she possessed to the end of her life the fortifying of hope. Just as her dear Dean Swift could enable Queen Anne to enjoy "the credit of extending her bounty" to the Church of Ireland, Averil Corfe enabled the

South of England to extend its bounty to the often dismissed and galling coal-smeared face of the North-East of England. She could evoke, somehow without causing shame, Cunninghame-Graham's eulogy to the great socialist Keir Hardie:

> On foot and in the tramways, but mostly on foot, converged long lines of men and women. Yet there was something in the crowd that showed it was to attend no common funeral. No one wore black, except a minister or two, who looked a little like the belated rook you sometimes see amongst a flock of seagulls, in that vast ocean of gray tweed.
>
> They tramped along, the whistling north-east wind pinching their features, making their eyes run. The greater portion of the crowd were townsmen, but there were miners, washed, and in their Sunday best. Their faces showed the blue marks of healed-up scars into which the coal dust or gunpowder had become tattooed, scars gained in the battle of their lives down in the pits, remembrances of falls of rock or of occasions when the mine had "fired upon them."

" 'The blue marks of healed-up scars into which the coal dust or gunpowder had become tattooed.' " Yes. The words struck in her head as she was making herself coffee after that second night.

The morning post came. Averil got news that Tony had been involved in an accident while he was staying at a grand house in Yorkshire on a shoot. His Cambridge friend, depressed and overworked after exams, had put his gun to his mouth and blown his brains out. Tony, not noticing the terrible sight of his friend's brains on the ceiling and simply copying what he took to be a rich prank, pressed the trigger while he was cleaning the gun and permanently damaged his left eye. With surgery, his sight remained.

Harrow School

Dear Maman,

I have run out of shortbread and bull's eyes. I would like some more. Well done about the North.

Love,
Tony

Gosforth

Darling Tony,

It goes very unwell here. Miss Amy has taken another job as well as this one. She is helping to provide food at the welfare centres we have set up. I will do my best about the shortbread and the bull's eyes. Write to me about how you are, darling.

Love always,
Mummy

Harrow School

Dear Maman,

Something must have gone wrong because the shortbread and bull's eyes haven't arrived.

Tony
XXX

Gosforth

Darling Tony,

No, nothing has gone wrong except that there aren't any. Things are very bad up here. I expect a lot of your friends are involved in the Spanish Civil War and I am frightened for you because of your eye. You *mustn't* attempt such a thing. Please heed, I shall come South as soon as I can but I long for you to come North. There seem to have been so many school holidays when you haven't been able to. Don't worry.

Love always,
Mummy

Harrow School

Dear Maman,

There are plenty of bull's eyes and shortbread here. Hope you're well. We are all fine.

Tony
XXX

P.S. Don't get it about the Spanish Civil War. What about it? I'm too young and I'm physically impaired anyway.

Gosforth

Darling,

Here is a pamphlet about the Spanish Civil War. I think it makes good sense. I'm pinning a couple of pounds to this letter with a safety pin because there just aren't any bull's eyes or shortbread here. There's hardly a potato for haggerty. Do you remember haggerty? I hope so. You seem a long way away.

Love always,
Mummy

Harrow School

Dear Mater,

We can't get the kind of bull's eyes I like here so you will go on trying. Thanks loads etc. for the pocket money.

Your son,
Tony

Darling Tony,

I am sending some other biscuits and a few sweets of the sort you used to like. *Don't,* darling, feel that you have to go off to fight for the cause. You're not well enough, with your eye. Take great care of yourself.

Love always,
Mummy

Harrow School

Dear Mater,

Thank you loads for the other biscuits. I seem to have grown out of those sweets but there's another boy who likes them. Thank you for the pamphlet. It is very interesting.

Tony
XXX

Tony's skilled tact with his mother was so nicely unkind that it had to be denied the saving attribute of stupidity. His mother, by love goaded into long retorts, refrained. Her manner was always to be succinct and she supposed that her intimates—her father, her dead husband, her pleasing half-Tiresian son—would know her mode. Tony's moody sparring was quite foreign to her. It made her seem the stubborn one where she had always been told she was pliant. She disliked the moral bargaining that seemed to have become part of Tony's nature. And she wrote letter after letter to optical specialists about the chance of improving the sight of the damaged eye.

After writing one of them, and getting a null answer, she went to Blackpool on a Bank Holiday to see what was happening about the women's cause. Things had changed, of course. There were family groups everywhere with more shopping bags than children. The women often led the way, in bikinis and high-heeled shoes, bulging amiably as they fed potato crisps to the jammy-mouthed toddlers in the prams that their fathers were pushing while reading the *Daily Mirror*. Blue with cold around the edges of their bathing suits, the mothers carried bags from Marks & Spencer: their breasts, padded below with foam, looked as though they were meant to be used as boxers' punch bags, though seldom were a more kindly set of men accumulated behind any foray of prams. They, like Sir Douglass, were men who loved women. Their wives, exemplified in the beach postcards that had started in the genius of Donald McGill, were caricaturists' notions: nubile girls as plump as cushions, with flesh, you felt, that would quickly indent with the very first depression of the index finger, to expand again to its original boundless bulk. They were the object of unending loving jokes, solemn about small spending projects and the mothers-in-law of their quiescent, walnut-shaped husbands, who might, in the seaside-postcard tradition, spring out at them from behind a bathing hut or a deck chair with a perfectly terrible pun. They loved their husbands. They loved their impossibly envious mothers-in-law, because of this nut-sized source of joy in common. They gave succour and no grumbles to their husbands, and they gave lollipops, not rubber dummies or comforters, to their children, enthralled to be patting sand in no matter how high a wind. The piers, the famous seaside piers of England, stretched out into the sea like long arms bejewelled with rhinestone, strung up with lights in the evening, with penny-in-the-slot machines along their length and a beautiful Edwardian theatre at the end. Averil thought the women happy and beautiful. Even though she was living in a cheap lodging house where the ketchup was put beside the marmalade at breakfast time and cleared away at the same time as the guests, who were not allowed back by the landlady between ten o'clock in the morning and six in the evening, she thought that women had come a long way.

Harrow School

Chère Mater,

The chaps say you are at Blackpool. They say that Margate is for the newly wed or nearly dead. Which are you? Train fare must have cost you a fortune, too. The cost of living at Harrow is very high.

Tony
XXX

9

*A*veril decided then that the time had come to act. She brought Tony up North again: to see Braw Fell, to see Elsie and Bill, made redundant by Andrew's mother's death; to see Hilda, who had brought him up, all of them now living in her little house in Gosforth. Above all, she wanted him to see the shipyards that he would remember from happier times. Anything to flick the switch. Miss Amy, now much older, sustained her passion for ships and for the records of them. Perhaps that would be the needle of Tony's comatose memory. Such things can't be set up, of course, Averil thought, but Miss Amy scarcely runs against any of our North-East natures. Tony came into the old hut where Miss Amy sheltered with her records as if for the warmth that she provided for others with her strong hot coffee. Sir Douglass, now very old, was standing at the window of the hut watching for developments: lunch-break bells would go as usual, but this was the recession.

Miss Amy gave them coffee. "This will remind you of the Shah's visit. Oh, the pomp of it. And your grandmother and your dear aunt Lily. There they were in their sailor suits, and the Shah so chillsome, but polite as Royal Highnesses are. I believe he'd come begging for a loan, but this was before the First World War."

"I don't know about that much," said Tony. "It's not in School Certificate. Mamma keeps writing to me about not going to the Spanish Civil War, but I wouldn't dream of it; there's too much going on at school. Games and exams and things."

Miss Amy took some coffee for herself and said, "That must seem a long way away."

Sir Douglass said, "Tell him about what happened to the *Mauretania*."

"Well, there was this great launching, and then the war came, you see. She was requisitioned by the government."

"Hard cheese," said Tony.

"Gun mountings, all the armings of a transport ship in war-time. She took ten thousand to Gallipoli. In 1915 she was converted into a hospital ship and in 1918 helped to carry United States troops to France. Now she's going back to the North Atlantic. There'll be new outfittings because of us having gone all-out on the war."

"People at school say the Germans won, really," said Tony.

"No," said Sir Douglass, though he was looking at his own nearly deserted shipyard.

"Things are not as good now. But the North-East has always had its ups and downs. Our Mr. Marshall, a well-known figure in his own domain, was complaining that his yards were some-times like blasted forests. A wilderness of bare poles with the grass all too luxuriant. Well, we're used to the grass springing up when trade goes down. The funny thing is that the ship-building part, rich as it is in all these minerals and coal and water, also seems to be the most arable. You could keep a flock of sheep here when the orders aren't coming in. It's far more green here if times are like that than it is in the rest of North-umberland where the sheep are. There it tends to be heathery. You'll have seen the sheep I mean. Black-faced sheep, and very sturdy, proper Northumbrians. I'm sorry to introduce a sore note, but some of the men here are finding it difficult to adjust to the new forty-seven-hour week. They thought they wanted it but now some of them are saying they preferred the old fifty-four-hour week. My advice to them is it wasn't won without a fight and they're better off with a few hours extra to be with the family or help the missus and play the pipes with their mates. A lot of the men here had barely seen their bairns before the Act. The children were always asleep by the time they got home." Miss Amy looked to Sir Douglass for approval. His nod was implicit.

"Miss Amy, remind Tony of 1933. He'd have been South by then, but he'd remember it from my letters."

"I'm sure you keep all your mother's letters. Family memorabilia they are. I keep my mother's letters done up in pink ribbon like a barrister's brief. Well, last January was an especially cold one. You see the notes being kept here by Mr. Richard Hough. They're all exact, I can witness that. 'There were still three hours of winter darkness when the men on the day shift got up from their beds. They dressed in their woollen linings and trousers, under their two-piece overalls, and inevitable mufflers and caps, to the sound of the wind and the clatter of hobnail boots on the cobbles beneath their windows. Still unshaven, they let themselves out of their little brick terrace houses in Whitworth Street and Myrtle Place, Armstrong Road and Clara Street, and hurried downhill, guided by the widely spaced gas lamps. In Westmoreland Road, and close to the Elswick gates in Scotswood Road, brighter lights shining through patterns of stained glass drew the men toward the first comfort of their day. The pubs were legally permitted to open at six o'clock, five minutes before the works' gates were finally locked shut. The timing might have been designed to encourage speed and precision in the working men.' "

131

Amy broke off her reading, looked up, and said, "It certainly got the pub owners to offer the fastest service in the place. As six o'clock chimed out on the clocks, the doors were thrown open and the men poured in. Not much time for special orders. Neatly ranged along the bar were thick cups of strong tea and coffee and nips of rum or whiskey. Given scalded lips and throats there was just time for both. The debt was chalked up, I remember."

Miss Amy went back to reading Mr. Hough. " 'Then amid the sound of voices calling out in greeting and brief ribaldry, the men burst out into the darkness and ran toward the yard— to the bright lights and the thunder of machinery.' "

"Sounds fun," said Tony flatly.

Miss Amy said, "We've got a bad time ahead and a bad time behind us," declining to call Tony "sir," though his manner begged it. "The war's taken the spine out of the North-East because we did the best we could and it wasn't right. It was smaller ships that were wanted, not the big warships. In the war the Tyne, Wear, and Tees all together put out on the slipway one hundred and thirty ships of all sizes and descriptions. When the Armistice sounded, I'd have invested all I had in the *Mauretania*, but I'd have liked advice about what was next and there wasn't any advice coming. The yards were as busy as they'd ever been, with all the repairing and refitting because of the war. Any fool could tell it wouldn't last, but we didn't know where to turn. We got on with turbines, of course. We'd had to put out more and more tonnage because of the German submarines. 'Victory is now a question of tonnage, and the tonnage of Allied victory,' says Mr. Lloyd George. 'Nothing else can defeat us but a shortage of tonnage.' Well, fine words with the Welsh ring to them; the way he speaks always puts me in mind of a hymn, but where did that leave Tyneside in peacetime and where did that leave our family?"

132

"Where indeed, Tony? Eh?" said Sir Douglass.

"Making loot in the City," said Tony. "Or being idle if one's lost an eye. In my case."

Bill and Elsie tried to make a joke of some sort to Miss Amy. All of them left, including Hilda, under Averil's wing.

"A ruse to move the house away from Northumberland," said Averil out loud, predicting the nightmare she was to have years later in the builder's din of a London Georgian house.

10

Disturbed by Tony's nimble Harrovian cattiness, Averil let her house in Gosforth and came South. The Spanish Civil War had become Munich and the unforgettable waving of a piece of paper. "Peace in our time." Not easily with Tony. Tony went to Oxford and passed Classical Greats with a first. He married a wise and intelligent girlfriend of his childhood called Eliza, much like his mother, and went on to do nothing else for the rest of his misbegotten life but to make money through a seat at Lloyd's, have many mistresses, hunt, and play the cello, a gift for which he was much beloved by his son, to whom he once played it when Simon at three had earache. He had placed himself thoughtlessly behind Simon; Simon had to lie on the wrong side of himself, facing the fireplace, to let the ear drain. They were those sort of days. The sofa was a Knole one that kept him from the sight of his father. Eliza plugged on with her beloved friend, Mickey, who shared with her a fondness for cats. They went with Simon to the Olympia Cat Show. In front of a cage of beautiful Siamese, Mickey said, "They say the universe wasn't created by God but by boiling mud and clever bits of jelly and freakishly gifted little fishes. Well, here we are. Change ourselves." He clung to her arm and said, "How?"

135

Back at the house, Eliza sat in her dressing room and started to do her face. "It really would be easier—I think—if Tony were content. But he's only making do, and it doesn't seem enough for anyone. His girls are perfectly nice but he doesn't let them come anywhere near his mind. He treats them like checked luggage that a chauffeur is going to pick up."

Mickey said: "That's his choice. If it doesn't suit him, that's his problem."

"Like a fitted briefcase or a toolkit in a posh monogrammed bag."

Eliza looked grimly into the Edwardian shaving mirror. "In the old days it used to be difficult enough simply to find sex, didn't it? Ten or fifteen years ago? And there's so much of it now that it might as well be lying around in heaps on the streets, like bags of rubbish waiting to be collected by the City Council. Yet not much of it is any good, Tony seems to feel. Sometimes it's as if sex is something that goes on in a wood-burning fireplace, with him living in a smokeless zone. The house is full of secrets, and people seeing Tony think he's a genuine flaming fireplace but there's no bloody burn to it."

A cat they had bought at the Olympia Cat Show gazed at them like one of Tony's girls.

"What a nice afternoon. Cats like pipe cleaners and cats like those advertisements for fluffy white carpets and cats like those women who run stores at church fetes, and all behaving as if they're so grand. No, this one is quite amiably afflicted and slummy, I suppose. A misplaced eyeball and an expression like a wrecked Volkswagen. It looks like a fur coat that's been sold off in the railway lost-property office." Mickey picked up the cat, perhaps to make amends.

"I suppose I shouldn't say it, but Tony sounds a right hard one to me," said Mickey.

"I'm feeling impatient with his girls today. I don't know why this one doesn't leave him."

"It's not cowardice, I don't think."

"If it were, I'd know, because I'm a coward," Eliza said. "I'd also be much more angry with him. It always makes one angry to see one's own faults reflected. One's endlessly patient with the vices one doesn't happen to have."

"What was old Sir Douglass like? In your reading."

"He once went around the whole of the kingdom by boat. He was an engraver as a young man before he took to shipping. When I first went to Braw Fell with my parents—all of us were in shipping, all—I was allowed down to breakfast with the men because I was small enough not to have breakfast in bed on a tray, and he used to balance a penny in one of the cracks in the refectory table. It was a prize for me if I remembered not to tip the Cromwellian chair, which was pretty ropy. It was also a prize if I didn't splutter when he put a whole fried egg into his mouth when the men were behind *The Times*. It was an early test of control, you see, and of alliance. He was good at alliance. He was also very good at gadgets."

"I've heard about the hydraulic phaeton and your grandmother's wish for blue rhododendrons."

"Oh, no. Father went further than that. He dreamed of every improvement. Square eggs because they would be easier for packing. He kept a store of gummed utility labels that were meant to save envelopes for reuse in the Boer War and that he used on the furniture. He had very pretty handwriting. A Queen Anne left-hand drawer in the dressing room of one of his spare rooms had on it 'If this drawer appears to stick, don't despair. Pull it sharply to the right.' The cistern over the loo had a label on it saying, 'If this cistern should fail to pull in the middle of the night, don't despair. Wait three minutes and then pull again sharply. The door is double and you will not wake anyone.' He admired my mother very much and it took him a deal of courage to carry on his mind to work in the North after she died."

Mickey looked out of the window and said, "It was probably a mistake of mine to get a brother kitten to the one you've got. They'll miss each other."

"The breeder said cats don't. As soon as they've eaten and slept in a place, she says they're all right on their own."

"They can meet."

Mickey peered into the box containing the pedigree. "He's going to be masterful. I can see it. It's due to his forebears."

Eliza started laughing out of the window and Simon came into the drawing room.

"What is it now?" he said.

"It isn't actually a joke. I don't know what to do with it."

"Burn it," said Mickey. "Make margarine out of it."

"We've got all our cats in two baskets," said Eliza apologetically.

"*Mummy,*" said Simon. "She's very odd sometimes, isn't she?"

Elsie was cooking. Bill barged in.

"Well," he said, "so Mrs. Corfe's all right."

"What do you mean?"

"What are you doing?"

"What does it look like? Making us girdle cakes."

"I've got to wash the car. They're out tonight."

"Not on your nelly," she said. "She told me dinner for four with Simon downstairs and Nanny having it on a plate with the television because of her leg."

"What's the matter with her leg, then?"

"She carries on all the time about having a bone in her leg."

"She'd be in a pretty pickle if she didn't have *several* bones."

"It's a manner of speaking. Here's your girdle cakes."

"I told you, I haven't got time. I've got my obligations."

"This about the car. Mrs. Corfe was quite definite to me."

138

"Well, she's got another think coming. And there's a cat now too," said Bill. "Buying kittens they've been, she and her queer. Well, that's your lookout. I'm not carrying the litter up and down."

"Cat litter comes in the same category as logs, and logs is your job."

"Here. I'm working for him on loan. I'm going to stop carting the logs soon. Anyway, logs aren't permitted in S.W. 1. They're against the law. Smokeless zone, this is."

Elsie went on cooking. Bill said, "What are you doing?"

"Getting myself nice and ahead so you can have a bite on the early side and a sit-down with the papers."

Bill patted his stomach covertly and withdrew further into coldness.

"Bill Watson, you're not stout," said Elsie. "You never were."

"Stop dwelling on the past. We're in London now."

"You're telling me."

"I just don't fancy anything to eat with things as they are upstairs, that's all. Cheery up, hinney," he said, smacking her thighs proprietorially. She withdrew a little and laid her mistress's breakfast tray.

"As I've said again and again, what's the point of a hand-ironed serviette new every time when it's only Italian coffee and a piece of Kleenex would do."

Elsie went on cooking.

Bill said, "Can't you see it's irritating me?"

"Even if he's out, the others have got to eat."

"He's taking everyone in the house. It's a family party."

"I've heard that before. He says he will, and then it ends up with a boiled egg for her and Simon at a dance."

"Please yourself. Anyway, it's not dances now, that's all over. It's discotheques. Pitch dark, no booze, your girl a yard away from you when you're dancing, and a load of noisy strangers two inches away from you when you're sitting down. Not my idea of where to go if you're a member of the privileged classes."

"How can it be a family party if she's there?"

"Who?"

"That Georgina."

"Nice girl."

"My madam puts up with a lot."

"Table's been booked for three weeks, and it's in madam's name because she's the member, so she's got to go."

Bill went out of the kitchen and they carried on talking in shouts.

Bill yelled, at the sounds of cooking, "You're still at it, aren't you?"

"I don't fancy having to start this lot all over again." She paused. "You know what, they're messing us around."

"What?"

"I said they're messing us around."

"That's what I've kept telling you. Stop putting yourself out for her. You don't pay me no heed."

"It's only her," said Elsie. "You put yourself out for him."

"He pays the wages, doesn't he? Mine *and* yours."

"That wasn't called for." Pause for cooking. "That was crude to her *and* to me."

"Belt up," Bill yelled from the back door. Elsie sat down at the kitchen table wretchedly and then got up to carry on.

In the dressing room, Tony Corfe looked with suspicion at the cat box. "What are you going to do with it?"

"What does one usually do with kittens?"

Eliza was silent.

"Drown them with bricks in a sack at birth," said Tony.

140

"You remind me of the rich little boy who used to amuse himself pulling the wings off houses."

"I don't get it."

"No, I hoped you wouldn't." Pause. "I like you most of all when you're obtuse. Your board meetings have made you rather alert."

Tony looked glazed and tied an Ascot knot in his tie.

"You do that very well," said Eliza.

"My Mamma doesn't think so."

"You never think anyone thinks well of you."

Downstairs, Billl said, out of sight of Elsie, "Now what? You're still at it. Don't tell me. And stop looking so wretched."

"It doesn't seem right. Not when she doesn't know it's off. She had it all planned. She was looking forward to it. You're counting on its being off, and that's not our business, is it? She might still make him change his mind."

"Make me a cuppa," said Bill. Elsie accepted the olive branch and stood with her hand on the television set, making for the kettle, waiting for it to start to boil. "Football's on the news." He came in and looked at what was in the saucepan.

"Go on, you have a bit," said Elsie.

"You know I don't before I'm going to drive."

"I didn't mean that, I meant the cassoulet. It's a deal of trouble, a cassoulet, pig's trotters and salami and all over Soho, but she fancied it."

"He doesn't."

"Chances are she'll be eating it by herself."

"That Nanny doesn't."

"A lightly boiled egg and thin toast and margarine to get Simon used to Eton. Eton sounds like Wormwood Scrubs or Alcatraz to me."

"What's Alcatraz?"

"The prison people can't escape from. They say it costs as much as Eton, and no extras."

"I thought extras was in at Eton."

"Only boating and double Greek."

"You learn a lot."

"Not from that Nanny. Simon tells me when we go shopping."

Back in the dressing room, Tony again glanced at the scuffling cat box and said, "No cat of mine is going to go around in cardboard."

"It'll be a proper box tomorrow, but one needs to wait two weeks to make sure it's disinfected from the old cat."

"Why not get a new one?"

"This is a new cat."

"I mean a new box."

"You can never be sure." Eliza, feeling dismal but bent on not being dispirited, sprang around the dressing room singing again "Everything under one roof," the jingle written on buses to advertise a shop that offered you an elephant in five days should you need one, or a mattress in much less, and thought of the people under her roof. Simon, her adrift Simon; Tony, who refused to use what sight he still had on the gifts he had always very much possessed; Averil, bent on her quarterly train journeys to the North-East; Bill and Elsie, not as happy as they had been.

"What are you going to do with it?" said Tony.

"With what?"

"The cat."

"What do you mean? What do people usually do with cats?"

"Breed them, don't they? Use them as doorstops. I don't know. I think it's giving me hay fever. Did you buy it on purpose to give me hay fever?"

"Yes, of course. Do you want some antihistamine pills?"

"Yes."

Eliza knelt down in front of a cupboard under his washbasin.

"What would you like better," she said, "antihistamine pills or butterscotch?"

"It depends on whether I've got hay fever or not, rather naturally." He paused with dignified interest. "Do you mean there is any butterscotch?"

"In your drawer."

She went into the bedroom and said from there, "Oh, what a good day."

Tony gave a complicated sneeze, possibly self-induced. "What's good about it?"

Eliza shouted from the bedroom, "When you break your diet it's always a good sign, I've found."

"You've spoiled my appetite." Tony had no humour in him about such things: this was a complaint. "I don't want it so early, thank you."

"What do you mean, at half-past ten?" She came back into the room. "It's awfully *late* for Elsie."

She gave him the butterscotch. He would have liked to eat it, but self-esteem forbade. "We're dining here," she said on a question mark.

"We're dining out."

"Oh." Disappointment, apprehension, peril. She turned away. "Who?"

"You and me," Tony said. "I've got an American to entertain."

"Oh, work. I'd better go up and explain to Ma we won't be in after all. What do you want me to say to her?"

"I'm taking her too. I'm taking everyone. I thought it might be amusing."

"Well, I must still tell her we're not dining here, because

she'll want to change. They'll never let Simon in, though. Will they? You did mean him too?"

Tony said vaguely, elusively, "It would be pretty late for him anyway."

"Tony, it is his long leave. He won't be home again for six weeks. I tell you what. I'll stay behind and take him to the flicks instead or something. Though I suppose you can't really deal with a businessman and your Ma alone today. She's not very well."

"I'll tank her up with sherry or something. There'll be plenty of other people there to take the weight off her. But you've got to come, now I think of it. It's your membership."

Eliza took an unusually frozen pause. "Well," she said firmly, "then you explain to Nanny that she's got to find something nice for Simon to do. We could send him to the theatre with a mate. No, it wouldn't be much fun. We can't have him spending his long leave with Frank going on about the bone in her leg."

"Good Christ, it's only one evening. There are three more. And who on earth is Frank?"

"Nanny. I've been calling her Frank to myself because she's always saying she can't help being frank about everything. When it's the last thing she is, frank."

"Frank about what?"

"Oh, I don't know."

"About what?"

"Darling, she's not that stupid."

"What have you said to her?"

"I haven't said anything."

"You must have done. I regard that as unforgivable of you. What does she know?"

"Feelings, I should think. People do."

Tony threw an expensive shaving brush at the bathroom looking glass and broke both.

144

"Tony," said Eliza, "she doesn't know anything about your private business or your all-too-public affairs. She doesn't know more about Mickey than she sees, for that matter. Except that you're hardly ever here and that I hardly know anything about you any longer. It must be plain even to Nanny that we've lost one another somewhere. And now I suppose she'll know your bombshell about us, because I'm not going to be secretive about it. That's my decision."

"You'll have upset her. She's my Nanny."

"But it won't have upset you. If only it had." She paused. "Why should it upset Nanny?"

"I just know it will. You've never got on with her and it's always been the devil of a job for me to keep the situation pinned together."

"For you?"

"As I said, she's my Nanny."

"And very proud of you."

"It's not like you to be sarcastic."

"You must be out of your mind. You've hardly entered the situation. She's always been here because of Simon and because of wanting to hang on to the memory of you when you were Simon's age. And it's always worked perfectly well as long as I've stayed out of her hair and never shown her what I thought, and stayed out of competition with her and Simon, and let her feel superior about knowing far, far more about you than I do, which is even possibly true, and that's the pang of it. And now I'm getting serious and I shall probably start on what you sweetly call a crying jag, one of the things you despise me for, so let's pretend none of it is happening and that I'm not stupidly disappointed not to be having an evening alone at home with you, which I'm not any longer, and we'll have a nice time papering the cracks. A nice party, I mean. Is there any such thing as a nice party?"

Speaking rapidly to herself in what she knew to be an unheard monologue, she caught the sound of her infant husband going up the stairs and shouting "Nan-ny." The two falling notes he must have used when he was four years old. She followed him up the stairs and said to the old woman in front of Tony, energized, "Simon, watch television with Nanny and go to bed at ten. We're going out unfortunately and it'll all be talk about cheap money, whatever that may be. I've always thought money was extremely expensive." She paused and said more firmly than usual, "I mean, Nanny, that Simon is not to go out this evening. It will be an inappropriate place."

Down in the drawing room, Eliza found Tony ineptly entertaining his businessman, with Lady Corfe looking out of the window, as she so often did in her grown-up son's presence. Tony turned to Eliza and said, "Right, it's nearly eight. I'll pick up you and Ma and our good friend in a couple of hours, at ten-fifteen, say."

Eliza said, "But what about dinner? Aren't we to have dinner together? Elsie's already had something with Bill and I thought they had the evening off."

Tony said, "Our good friend told me he's got to dine with a friend for a couple of hours."

The businessman, a sensitive one, called Mr. Winston, said, "I said I would have a bite with another very good friend of mine."

Tony copied his speech pattern and said, "That's right. He said he would have a bite with a very good friend of his."

Eliza said, "Anyway, I don't think Ma's coming. She said she wanted to go to bed with a Bath Oliver water biscuit."

Tony said, "Well, it might be a blessing in disguise."

Eliza gave him a glance. "Mr. Winston, do you want a taxi?"

Tony said, "Why don't you drive him yourself in your car? I need Bill." He moved to a window yards from his mother and

146

waited for Mr. Winston to get up. He did, and said to Eliza, "That's very kind of you and I'd certainly appreciate it." Awkwardness reigned. Tony sprang away from the window and said, "Sorry, I've got to desert you. See you anon with my lady wife."

Eliza took Mr. Winston downstairs and looked back at the room, wondering how the reshuffle could have happened and where Tony meant to go while she was away. She drove Mr. Winston to his dinner, which turned out to be at a hamburger place with a blaring discotheque, and then wandered about Leicester Square, read an evening paper by the neon lights of a cinema, and went to a phone box to ring Nanny. "Nanny, could I speak to Simon? . . . Oh. Then he must have gone out in spite of what . . . No, don't worry, I'm sure Mr. Corfe would have found out where he was going."

11

In a noisy nightclub called The Steam Bath, where laser beams played across the top, and fog made of dry ice and looking much like smog covered the remote dancers up to their waists, Eliza gave her things to the hat-check girl. She hated the place but Tony had persuaded her to join it and given her the membership fee almost as though it were pocket money. She stayed there for a long time. A man alone at a table opposite, just visible from the waist upward above the smog, had also left his coat and eaten his way through a very large and expensive meal. When he got up and collected his coat he gave the girl a five-pence bit. She said, "Thanks." Terseness for stinginess.

Eventually Tony and Mr. Winston arrived. Lady Corfe was with them, as Eliza had sensed. It was a troublesome and noisy evening. The dry ice seemed to have entered the rather unpleasant large steaks. Lady Corfe wrote a note to Eliza in her usual clear handwriting, reading, "I believe Georgina is here. I can't see in this fog. I think Tony has brought Simon in spite of all you said." Eliza folded the note and put it into her evening bag. After the fog-ridden steak—"the level of air pollution is unacceptable today," as the jaunty weather reports so often say, though how does one not accept air?—Eliza got up and said

149

that she was going to the loo. There were two doors, one drawn with something like a Dutch doll and the other with a womanly-looking person wearing trousers. As all the girls around were wearing such trousers, Eliza was not sure which door to make for. She suddenly heard Tony's voice. And he said impatiently, "I'm going. You know I've got an appointment. Do whatever you want. I don't mind. You have got enough money for a taxi?"

A voice all too certainly Georgina's said, "Yes, thanks."

Tony said, "I wish you wouldn't look at me like that all the time."

Georgina's soprano voice said, "Sorry."

"You look so reproachful. I can't help it if you haven't enjoyed yourself. There were plenty of people here you knew."

Georgina's meekened voice again: "I'm sorry. I don't mean to look anything. I have enjoyed it, really."

"For heaven's sake stop saying you're sorry."

"I'll go now, shall I?"

The two walked out, and the voice was not Georgina's but Simon's. Eliza hit Tony and ran through the sophisticated fog to Averil.

Averil saw the predicament that had happened in this witlessly jocular place that lacked any admission of the past or any that people might be more intelligent than the times assessed them to be.

"Tony, enough," leaving her hand near his. Other years, the same purposes. He was so dead silent, looked so bewildered, that she went on to say, "What's up, old son?" and gave him a breadstick dampened by the false fog, spreading butter in encouraging lumps on it. He ate it as though he hadn't had anything else for weeks. The Harrow bacon he shoved in time-honoured way under the table to the murmured travesty of a particularly hated hymn, "The daily rind, the common task,

150

will furnish all we need to ask"; "rind" being "grind" in the chastened English public-school mind, to lighten. Cold baths, enforced runs, the early-morning chapel: pretenses of the reality of hardship, as Averil saw it with sympathy, and as Tony, the apparently clean-cut mutant, seemed to feel it. She longed to hold him in some laconic way that would pass on the sagacity that would die with her, but embraces say little enough to humans and probably only scarcely more to cats. So she made the move from the table so curiously riddled with expensive false fog, shook it off her dress and her grandson's clothes (not icicles, but chemical remnants), and took him home. His home, perhaps, though he was farmed out from both his London house and from the Alcatraz/Wormwood Scrubs of an expensive public school that treated its pupils as muddled disciples of a Raj that had done its job and of a new order of computer analysts. What, Averil asked of Simon on the way back to the big house, was a computer analyst?

"I find analysts of human beings hard enough to follow. Founded on the expenditure of a great deal of money being 'good' for their so-called patients. It always amuses me that spending money, hard-earned money, should be called good for patients. Better for the receiver, eh?" She opened the window of Tony's car so that Bill should hear, and said, "You have by me Mr. Corfe's permission to crank that window between us down. It's not as though we were in a bulletproof car. And in any case, bulletproofing promotes the random. The random assassin seeking celebrity. Do you know the width of a tube platform in Manhattan, Bill?"

"Asking for a madman shover," said Bill.

"Have you read about the children at an expensive American school where the boys were equipped with computers and no knowledge of what they were for, though every mechanical know-how of what to do, and managed in their infinite spare time to connect their computers to many others in many other places that they traced to be banks offering competitive tax-free electric blenders or what-not for ten thousand dollars' deposit and thereby also managed to lose, to *lose*, displace, not to thieve, thirteen billion dollars?"

"It was on television," said Bill. "I don't care for the weather forecasts. If I had the money and the child—no, let's get it right, the child and the money—nothing in the world would get me to send him or her to one of those expensive public-school prison camps. They're lonely."

"Yes, and also now aware that time runs more keenly in loneliness," said Averil. "So where would you say the brilliance of North-East shipbuilding lay? Began?"

"In William Armstrong, Charles Palmer, perhaps another score, and your grandfather and husband."

"Some of them were born in the North-East; some by fortune or ear-tune arrived in the area."

"Ear-tune. Now, there's a happy phrase," said Bill.

"Grandma tunes the harpsichord," said Simon.

"That's not what we meant," said Averil.

"I *know*," said Simon. "And I *know* Mamma took my voice in the loo for some girl's. Papa only took me in there for company."

"Company?"

"I've got an American friend called Elsie," said Simon. "Not our Elsie. The American Elsie worked for all sorts of people. She worked for bandleaders. She and her husband. He was the chauffeur. Both being black. She worked for my father once in America. He didn't know what she meant by 'passed.' I've heard my father say it about Mickey Shaw. But in other places it means racial, doesn't it? And my father couldn't understand how she was wearing Chanel clothes. But they'd been handed on to her, you see, by her bandleader friends, and they were a good fit."

"And she could 'pass'?"

"She didn't care about it because she worked."

"And she still does?" said Bill.

"I had a card from her, a Christmas card, well ahead of time, saying she was 'lazy or tired.'"

"She's eighty-two. She lives in Virginia," said Elsie. "Her grandparents would have been slaves."

"She said she was lazy because she'd had company that hunting season in Virginia. Cooking for forty-one in the family. Her husband, aged eighty, has just died of what he called the sweats. She misses him."

"He was the one who used to sit in front of television all day and who'd been told he had to walk?" said Averil.

"She walked him. She walked him after work," said Simon. "She worked from six in the morning until six at night and then she walked him to get rid of the sweats."

"It would have been high blood pressure?" said Bill. "Searing pain or a dull ache?"

"Your friend would have found it a searing agony in her husband, whatever he called it. Doctors are busy and they don't listen," said Averil.

"Elsie says she has to come down from the bedroom in Virginia at four in the morning and can't get back to sleep for wondering why she's tired. That's what she says on her postcard. I can't tell you all of it, some of it's private," said Simon. "It was actually a Christmas card, of course, but sent far in advance. For fear of the mails, you see."

"For fear of the mails?" said Bill.

"She told me she'd sent seven Christmas cards already this year and got eight. She said she used to—she spelled it 'useter,' knowing I believe in spelling 'Shakespeare' 'Shakspere'—send up to three hundred and get back up to four hundred. Then she useter send up to one hundred but she says that was in the days when a card cost only two cents. She said she useter work

153

in the mails. She delivered letters. I think she's getting a bit tired now. That's what her writing looks like."

"Darling," said Averil, "your mother's cousin, your first cousin twice removed, went on the march called the Jarrow March. There were fears that the unemployed men on the march would not be physically fit enough. Before such an ordeal. All the way from Durham and Northumberland to London. All the men taking part were medically examined. As a matter of fact, they ate better during the march than they had done for many a year. There was not one out of the two hundred that did not put on weight and look and feel better than at the beginning. The march was expensive. It grew to thousands. It was estimated that the cost of feeding each man was four pounds, with another total of one hundred and fifty pounds to hire a train to bring them back."

"I've heard of the Aldermaston antibomb marches," said Simon.

"Then it was unemployment. Now it's nuclear war. What one American President always called 'nucular.' He also said the 'nucular family.' One husband, one wife, one son, one daughter."

"How dull," said Simon. "Though as it happens, I'd rather like to have a sister."

"To go back to the Jarrow March, and it was much the same thing as the Aldermaston March about nuclear weapons . . ."

Bill stopped the car in St. James's Park to listen.

"The marchers set off on Monday, October 5, 1936. Practically the whole town turned out to see the start. A few women cried, but it was for fear of seeing their men go to the South. The local press didn't like it. 'We have no liking for this event. At the present season it involves a risk to those taking part that might well have been avoided. It can only be hoped that the appeal they bear to Parliament will receive the consideration it undoubtedly deserves.' Tame stuff, considering that newspapers are traditionally written by radicals and owned by Tory know-alls and land-smirchers."

"Why are you going on like this?"

"Because you're better off, being younger than I am," said Averil, "but worse off, also, being younger in an era of youth ghettos that hasn't much sense of the past. I met a man yesterday who didn't know the difference between Alger Hiss and Rudolf Hess."

"I don't."

"No, but you will if you read. I read Gibbon's *Decline and Fall of the Roman Empire* when I was a small child because it was on the lowest shelf of my father's library and that's present history. Read Defoe's *History of the Plague Year*. He wrote it sixty years after the Great Plague, but one wouldn't know it because as well as being a great investigative reporter, he was such a great fiction writer. The two things aren't antithetical. Not at all. Read your own family history. It will tell you everything."

"About Georgina, even?"

"No, she would be a new instance. But you have to give it to her that she's pretty. And necessary, I suppose."

Simon paused and then said firmly, "I think she's gross, obnoxious, and weird."

"Find three other words, darling."

"Then 'weird.'"

"I think you were asking before about your Mamma."

"She's not weird."

"Not at all. She just holds her hush."

Back at the big house, they found Tony struggling with his own door key. Bill parked and got out to help.

"It's the wrong one, sir."

"Someone's jammed the chain inside."

"Sir, the light's bad, but this isn't the right key."

"I've got so many keys to different houses and my offices that I don't know where I am." Again that look that Averil had found affecting in the nightclub. "I feel a hoax, Bill. Excuse me."

"This key you were using is marked with nail polish, sir. It wouldn't be your office key. Your office key is here, sir. You've got them all safely." Bill opened the door for Tony and went down to the basement. The right key, at once. The suited small lantern over the basement door to see it by. Elsie was asleep. She had left a tray for him: a thermos flask of cocoa, a Northumberland scone, and butter and a honeycomb.

"Devonshire honey, dove," said Bill to Elsie, having taken the tray into their bedroom.

"It's all the same now. It's even French butter. The Common Market."

"We were sold a false bill of goods. Did we vote? In the referendum?" said Bill.

"I did. You were driving."

"A wife should have her husband's proxy," said Bill steadily.

"I don't see how. Suppose they had different views and cheated. Like His Nibs might."

"Dangerous ground, old darling. What was that I was saying about the Common Market?"

"You'll be saying next when you read a menu, you'll be asking *me*, 'Do I like pizza?' You've got your own memory bank."

"Bye, hinny, and when haven't you been it?" said Bill.

"Get back to the false bill of goods."

"England was told it was going to provide a storehouse of historical wisdom to plough into united Europe, and all we've done is join a rich men's club of countries and not know a blind thing about Chile or assassinating the Pope, trying to assassinate him, or tell a plot from the act of some barmy loner."

"And send up the price of food and save on schoolbooks. Simon's kept his bearings. He's found a cheaper way to go to France if you pretend to go by Brussels and just don't take the connection in Paris. Waste of petrol, but it saves him money and the airlines wait to fill up the planes anyway. He's going canoeing on the Loire."

"Mister doesn't know."

"But Mrs. Corfe does."

Rock had been hit between them.

"I wonder if we're going to get through this," said Elsie. "We should find another job, perhaps. But after all these years. And a job is a job."

"We can stick it out easily enough. It's not exactly like a famine in India yet."

"Your chauffeur's ulcer is on a knife edge, I can tell. Bus drivers get them. It's the loneliness. That bit of plastic between you and the passengers. Give me a bike any day."

"Lady Corfe wanted the glass pulled down tonight. She always does. It's not plastic yet, by the way, any more than we've come to bulletproof buses. Bulletproofing leads to a lot of bullets, like Tony."

And up above, Averil Corfe and Mickey Shaw and Eliza and Tony were together in the drawing room. Averil's head was bent, though she was standing upright in front of the fireplace.

"She's thinking," said Mickey.

"She's asleep on her feet, or writing one of her old pamphlets," said Tony.

Averil's head shot up and she said, "Tony, don't you see? To take your girlfriend out like that would have been bad enough. To take Simon to that smog place when Eliza had specifically said no is worse. Yes, it's terrible about your eye, but more terrible to have thought you were copying a prank and not to

157

have noticed that your friend had blown his brains out. His brains, Tony. Don't you remember the shipyards at all?"

"You *are* writing a pamphlet. One of your old clippings. Gone yellow."

"You've no memory of the past. Oh, my dear. It's the blight of the time. You won't remember Miss Amy. Your grandfather's secretary. Her clippings about the ships we'd built were like a family tree. She worked in something called the Shed. A sort of title. Much like a Nissen hut, but you won't remember that either, because Nissen huts were in the war before last, before the Vietnam war, and you only seem to know the present. Even Oxford lost to you. I suppose you do that because the future is unthinkable."

Tony held his blind eye.

"Yes, darling, but that was because you didn't ever think about the supposedly unthinkable. Didn't bother. Go back to the shipyards. Thirty thousand trained men out of work on Tyneside alone. The grass growing in the yards again. The victuallers forgotten. Since I made the mistake of sending you to jumped-up Harrow far from home, because you wanted it, I don't supposed you even know how to say 'victuallers,' let alone what they do. To hell with a first in Classical Greats. What about a not very modern and not very great government that fights the Falkland Islands war?"

"It was a splendid war, Mamma, and it's given backbone to a lot of people. You should have seen the Stock Exchange floor."

"Those ships lost."

"Those men," said Eliza.

"Same thing," said Averil.

"The seamen," said Tony.

"And what about the men out of work who built the ships in the first place?" said Averil. To Mickey, about a sherry, "Ta ever so, but not now. *Aië aië aië. 'Pourvu qu'ils y tiennent':* if

158

only they hold on, the French newspapers said in the Great War about Verdun. But what have these men now got to hold on to? A contract to rebuild the ships we lost in a fabricated war. The contract was put out to tender and Korea got it. The British government thought the contract should go to Tyneside, but what does that accomplish? Eighteen months' work and then the dole again. The Tyneside estimate was three times the Korean one."

"Natch," said Tony.

"Naturally," said Averil. Pause. "A jingo war to give men jobs? Costing the government that went to war for poor reasons a mint that it hasn't got?"

Averil sat down on a footstool and rested her chin on her hands, her cane between her knuckles, as if it were her better limb.

"You've got a chin like a baby's heel," said Eliza.

"Onward," said Averil to Tony. "Remember Miss Amy when you can. Remember Aunt Lily collecting stones. When we all are trapped like birds in a cage—"

"—We'll laugh, and pray, and tell old tales," said Eliza.

"Lily might have been planning to build Stonehenge, for all I know," said Averil. "I wonder what any of us has in mind?"

Note

Having grown up in a background of ancestral Northumberland, of the growth of shipbuilding and coal-mining and broadsheet-writing, and of the North-East's continuing acumen and courage, my thanks are due to centuries of family papers and records, and particularly to the following books and documentary sources. I have also scrounged my own piece, published in the magazine *Grand Street* and called "Northumberland, the Unknown County," with the grace of the editor, Ben Sonnenberg. So, the books:

The History of North-East Shipbuilding by David Dougan, *The Town That Was Murdered* by Ellen Wilkinson, *Women on the Warpath* by David Mitchell, *Jonathan Swift* by Nigel Dennis, *Votes for Women* by Roger Fulford, *Unshackled* by Dame Christabel Pankhurst, *Memories of a Militant* by Annie Kenney, *Keir Hardi* by Kenneth D. Morgan, *Power on Land and Sea* by Joseph F. Clark, *Keir Hardie* by Emrys Hughes, *The Baldwin Age* edited by John Raymond, *Woman's Suffrage* by Helen Blackburn, *Charles Kingsley* by Brenda Colloms, *Portrait of Northumberland* by Nancy Ridley, *Northern England* by The Rt. Hon. Lord Harlech, *Keir Hardie (The Making of a Socialist)* by Fred Reid; and *A Worker's History of the Great Strike* by R. W. Postgate, Ellen Wilkinson, M. B. and J. F. Horrabin.